Dearest Reader,

Welcome to the town of Hard Luck, Alaska! I hope you'll join me there to meet the Midnight Sons, their families, friends and wives-to-be.

The people I want to credit with the idea for this project are, in fact, fictional—they're Valerie, Stephanie and Norah, the three sisters I wrote about in the Orchard Valley trilogy (Harlequin Romance #3232, #3239, #3244). I loved writing those books, I loved the characters and the town and last but definitely not least, I loved the way readers responded to the stories.

So when Harlequin suggested this six-book project, I was thrilled. Soon after that, the town of Hard Luck, the O'Halloran brothers and Midnight Sons all came to life. Never have I worked harder on a project, nor have I enjoyed my research more. In the summer of 1994, my husband and I traveled to Alaska, and I fell in love with the state—its sheer magnificence, the warmth of its people, the excitement of life on the "last frontier."

Now I invite you to sit back, put your feet up and allow me to introduce you to some proud, stubborn, *wonderful* men—Alaskan men—and show you what happens when they meet their real matches. Women from the "lower forty-eight." Women with the courage to change their lives and take risks for love. Women a lot like you and me!

Love,

Debbie

Debbie Macomber is one of the most popular romance authors writing today. She's written more than seventy romances (for Harlequin and Silhouette) and several bestselling "mainstream" women's fiction novels. Not surprisingly, Debbie has won a number of awards for her books.

She lives in Washington State with her husband, Wayne, and their dog, Peterkins. They have four grown children—and they've just become grandparents! Debbie's *thrilled* with her new granddaughter, Jazmine Lynn.

Debbie loves to hear from her readers. You can reach her at: P.O. Box 1458, Port Orchard, Washington 98366.

Books by Debbie Macomber

HARLEQUIN ROMANCE

3232—VALERIE *(Orchard Valley trilogy)*
3239—STEPHANIE *(Orchard Valley trilogy)*
3244—NORAH *(Orchard Valley trilogy)*
3271—LONE STAR LOVIN'
3288—READY FOR ROMANCE
3307—READY FOR MARRIAGE

Midnight Sons is a six-book series. The titles are:

3379—BRIDES FOR BROTHERS (October 1995)
3383—THE MARRIAGE RISK (November 1995)
3387—DADDY'S LITTLE HELPER (December 1995)
3395—BECAUSE OF THE BABY (February 1996)
3399—FALLING FOR HIM (March 1996)
3403—ENDING IN MARRIAGE (April 1996)

Don't miss any of our special offers. Write to us at the following address for information on our newest releases.

Harlequin Reader Service
U.S.: 3010 Walden Ave., P.O. Box 1325, Buffalo, NY 14269
Canadian: P.O. Box 609, Fort Erie, Ont. L2A 5X3

MIDNIGHT SONS
DEBBIE MACOMBER

Daddy's Little Helper

Harlequin Books

TORONTO • NEW YORK • LONDON
AMSTERDAM • PARIS • SYDNEY • HAMBURG
STOCKHOLM • ATHENS • TOKYO • MILAN
MADRID • WARSAW • BUDAPEST • AUCKLAND

ISBN 0-373-03387-7

DADDY'S LITTLE HELPER

First North American Publication 1995.

Printed in U.S.A.

The History of Hard Luck, Alaska

Hard Luck, situated fifty miles north of the Arctic Circle, near the Brooks Range, was founded by Adam O'Halloran and his wife, Anna, in 1931. Adam came to Alaska to make his fortune, but never found the gold strike he sought. Nevertheless, the O'Hallorans and their two young sons, Charles and David, stayed on—in part because of a tragedy that befell the family a few years later.

Other prospectors and adventurers began to move to Hard Luck, some of them bringing wives and children. The town became a stopping-off place for mail, equipment and supplies. The Fletcher family arrived in 1938 to open a dry goods store.

When World War II began, Hard Luck's population was fifty or sixty people, all told. Some of the young men, including the O'Halloran sons, joined the armed services; Charles left for Europe in 1942, David in 1944 at the age of eighteen. Charles died during the fighting. Only David came home—with a young English war bride, Ellen Sawyer (despite the fact that he'd become engaged to Catherine Fletcher shortly before going overseas).

After the war, David qualified as a bush pilot. He then built some small cabins to attract the sport fishermen and hunters who were starting to come to Alaska; he also worked as a guide. Eventually, in the early seventies, he built a lodge to replace the cabins— a lodge that later burned.

David and Ellen had three sons, born fairly late in their marriage—Charles (named after David's brother) was born in 1960, Sawyer in 1963 and Christian in 1965.

Hard Luck had been growing slowly all this time, and by 1970 it was home to just over a hundred people. These were the years of the oil boom, when the school and community center were built by the state. After Vietnam, ex-serviceman Ben Hamilton joined the community and opened the Hard Luck Café, which became the social focus for the town.

In the late 1980s, the three O'Halloran brothers formed a partnership, creating Midnight Sons, a bush-pilot operation. They were awarded the mail contract, and also deliver fuel and other necessities to the interior. In addition, they serve as a small commuter airline, flying passengers to and from Fairbanks and within the north Arctic.

At the time these stories start, there are approximately 150 people living in Hard Luck—a preponderance of them male....

CHAPTER ONE

THE NEW SCHOOLTEACHER wouldn't last.

It didn't take Mitch Harris more than five seconds to make that assessment. Bethany Ross didn't belong in Alaska. She reminded him of a tropical bird with its brilliant plumage. Everything about her was *vivid,* from her animated expression to her sun-bleached hair, which fell to her shoulders in a frothy mass of blond. Even blonder curls framed her strong, classic features. Her eyes were a deep, rich shade of chocolate.

She wore a bright turquoise jumpsuit with a wide yellow band that circled her trim waist. One of her skimpy multicolored sandals dangled from her foot as she sat on the arm of Abbey and Sawyer O'Halloran's sofa, her legs elegantly crossed.

This get-together was in her honor. Abbey and Sawyer had invited the members of the school board to their home to meet the new teacher.

To Mitch's surprise, she stood and approached him before he had a chance to introduce himself. "I don't believe we've met." Her smile was warm and natural. "I'm Bethany Ross."

"Mitch Harris." He didn't elaborate. Details wouldn't be necessary because Ms. Ross simply wouldn't last beyond the first snowfall. "Welcome to Hard Luck," he said almost as an afterthought.

"Thank you."

"When did you get here?" he asked, trying to make conversation. He twisted the stem of his wineglass and watched the chardonnay swirl against the sides.

"I flew in this afternoon."

He hadn't realized she'd only just arrived. "You must be exhausted."

"Not really," she was quick to tell him. "I suppose I should be, considering that I left San Francisco early this morning. The fact is, I've been keyed up for days."

Mitch strongly suspected Hard Luck was a sorry disappointment to her. The town, population 150, was about as far from the easy California life-style as a person could get. Situated fifty miles north of the Arctic Circle, Hard Luck was a fascinating place with a strong and abiding sense of community. People here lived hard and worked harder. Other than Midnight Sons, the flight service owned and operated by the three O'Halloran brothers, there were a few small businesses, like Ben Hamilton's café. Mitch himself was one of a handful of state employees. He worked for the Department of the Interior, monitoring visitors to Gate of the Arctic National Park. This was in addition to his job as the town's public-safety officer—PSO—which meant he was responsible for policing in Hard Luck. Trappers wandered into town now and again, and an occasional pipeline worker. To those living on the edge of the world, Hard Luck was a thriving metropolis.

Lately the town had piqued the interest of the rest of the country, as well. But Bethany Ross had nothing to do with that. Thank heaven, although Mitch suspected she'd stay about as long as some of the women the O'Halloran brothers had brought to town.

Until recently only a small number of women had lived here. Not many were willing to endure the hardship of living this far from civilization. So the O'Hallorans had spearheaded a campaign to bring women to Hard Luck. Abbey was one of their notable successes, but there had been a few equally notable failures. Like—who was it?— Allison somebody. The one who'd lasted less than twenty-four hours. And only last week, two women had arrived, only to return home on the next flight out. Bethany Ross had actually applied for the teaching job last spring, though, before all this nonsense.

Unexpectedly she smiled—a ravishing smile that seemed to say she'd read his thoughts. "I plan to fulfill my contract, Mr. Harris. I knew what I was letting myself in for when I agreed to teach in Alaska."

Mitch felt the heat rise to his ears. "I didn't realize my... feelings were so transparent."

"I don't blame you for doubting me. I don't quite blend in with the others, do I?"

He was tempted to smile himself. "Hard Luck isn't what you expected, is it?"

"I'll adjust."

She said this with such confidence he began to wonder if he'd misjudged her.

"Frankly, I didn't know *what* to expect. With Hard Luck in the news so often, the idea of moving here was beginning to worry me."

Mitch didn't bother to conceal his amusement. He'd read what some of the tabloids had written about the town and the men's scheme to lure women north.

"My dad was against my coming," Bethany continued. "It was all I could do to keep him from flying up here with me. He seems to think Hard Luck's populated with nothing but love-starved bush pilots."

"He isn't far wrong," Mitch said wryly. If Bethany had only been in town a few hours, she probably hadn't met the pilots currently employed by Midnight Sons. He knew Sawyer had flown her in from Fairbanks.

It was after repeatedly losing their best pilots for lack of female companionship that the O'Hallorans had decided to take action.

"Midnight Sons is the flight service? Owned by the O'Hallorans?" she asked, looking flustered. "Sawyer and his brothers?"

"That's right." Mitch understood why she was confused. Immediately following her arrival, she'd been thrust into the middle of this party, with twenty names or more being thrown her way all at once. In an effort to help her, Mitch explained that Charles O'Halloran, the oldest of the three brothers, was a silent partner.

Charles, hadn't been so silent, however, when he learned about the scheme Sawyer and Christian had concocted to lure women to Hard Luck. He'd changed his tune, though, since meeting Lanni Caldwell. Earlier in the week, they'd announced their intention to marry.

"Is it true that Abbey—Sawyer's wife—was the first woman to come here?" Her eyes revealed her curiosity.

"Yes. They got married earlier this summer."

"But . . . they look like they've been married for years. What about Scott and Susan?"

"They're Abbey's children from a previous marriage. I understand Sawyer's already started the adoption process." Mitch envied his friend's happiness. Marriage hadn't been nearly as happy an experience for him.

"Chrissie's your daughter?" Bethany asked, glancing over at the children gathered around a Monopoly game.

Mitch's gaze fell fondly on his seven-year-old daughter. "That's right. She's been on pins and needles waiting for school to start."

Bethany's eyes softened. "I met her earlier with Scott and Susan. She's a delightful little girl."

"Thank you." Mitch tried hard to do his best for Chrissie. Sometimes he wondered, though, whether his best would ever be enough. "You've met Pete Livengood?" he asked, gesturing toward a rugged-looking middle-aged man on the other side of the room.

"Yes. He owns the grocery?"

"That's right. Dotty, the woman on his left, is another one who answered the advertisement."

Bethany blinked as if trying to remember where Dotty fit into the small community. "She's the nurse?"

He nodded. "Pete and Dotty plan to be married shortly. The first week of October, I believe."

"So soon?" She didn't give him an opportunity to answer before directing her attention elsewhere. "What about Mariah Douglas? Is she a recent addition to the town?"

"Yup. She's the secretary for Midnight Sons."

"Is she engaged?"

"Not yet," Mitch said, "but it's still pretty early. She only arrived last month."

"You mean to say she's lived here an entire month without getting married?" Bethany teased. "That must be some sort of record. It seems to me the virile young men of Hard Luck are slacking on their duties."

Mitch grinned. "From what I've heard, it isn't for lack of trying. But Mariah says she didn't come to Hard Luck looking for a husband. She's after the cabin and the twenty acres the O'Hallorans promised her."

"Good for her. They've fulfilled their part of the bargain, haven't they? I read that news story about the cabins not being anywhere close to the twenty acres. Sure sounds misleading to me." Fire flashed briefly in her eyes, as if she'd be willing to take on all three O'Hallorans herself.

"That's none of my business. It's between Mariah and the O'Hallorans."

Bethany flushed with embarrassment and bent her head to sip from her wine. "It isn't my business, either. It's just that Mariah seems so sweet and gentle. I hate the idea of anyone taking advantage of her."

They were interrupted by Sawyer and Abbey. "I see you've met Mitch," Sawyer said, moving next to Bethany.

"He's been helping me keep everyone straight," she said with a quick smile.

"Then he's probably told you that in addition to his job with the Department of the Interior, he's our public-safety officer."

"Hard Luck's version of the law," Mitch translated for her.

She leveled her gaze with his. "My father's a member of San Francisco's finest."

"Well," said Sawyer, "Mitch was one of Chicago's finest before moving here."

"That's right," Mitch supplied absently.

"I imagine your head's swimming right about now," Abbey said. "I know mine was when I first arrived. Oh—" she waved at a woman just coming in the door "—here's Margaret. Margaret Simpson, the high school teacher."

Margaret, a pleasant-looking brunette in her thirties, joined them. She greeted Bethany with friendly enthusiasm, explained that she lived on the same street as Sawyer and Abbey did and that her husband was a pipeline supervisor who worked three weeks on and three weeks off.

Mitch hardly heard the conversation between Margaret and Bethany; the words seemed to fade into the background as he found himself studying Bethany Ross.

He wanted to know her better, but he wouldn't allow himself that luxury. Although she claimed otherwise, he didn't expect her to last three months, not once the brutal winter settled in.

But still, she intrigued him. Tantalized him. The reasons could be as basic as the fact that he'd been too long without a woman—six years to be exact. He'd buried Lori when Chrissie was little more than an infant. Unable to face life on the Chicago police force any longer, he'd packed their bags and headed north. As far north as he could get. He'd known at the time that he was running away. But he'd felt he had no choice, not with guilt and his own self-doubts nipping at his heels. He was out of money and tired of life on the road by the time he reached Hard Luck.

And he'd been happy here. As happy as possible, under the circumstances. He and Chrissie had made a new life for themselves, made new friends. For Mitch, the world had become calm and orderly again, without pain or confusion. Without a woman in their lives.

He certainly hadn't anticipated meeting a woman like Bethany—a tropical bird—in Alaska.

She wasn't exactly beautiful, he decided. She was...striking. He struggled to put words to his assessment of her attributes. Feminine. Warm. Generous. Somewhat outrageous. Fun. The kids would love her. He'd spent ten, possibly fifteen, minutes chatting with her and immediately wanted more of her time, more of her attention.

But he refused to indulge himself. He'd learned all the lessons he ever wanted to learn from his dead wife. The new schoolteacher could tutor some other man.

Bethany yawned and tried to hide it behind the back of her hand.

"You must be exhausted," Abbey said sympathetically. "I can't believe we've kept you this long. I feel terrible."

"No, please, it was wonderful of you to make me feel so welcome." To her obvious chagrin, Bethany yawned again. "Maybe it would be best if I did leave now."

"She's dead on her feet," Sawyer said to no one in particular. "Mitch, would you be kind enough to escort her home?"

"Of course." He immediately set down his wineglass, but truth be known, he'd rather have declined. He was about to suggest someone else do the honor when he realized Bethany might find that insulting.

She studied him, and again he had the impression she could read his mind. He looked away and searched the room until he found his daughter. Chrissie was sitting near the door to the kitchen with her best friend, Susan. The two were deep in conversation, their heads close together. He didn't know what they were discussing, but whatever it was seemed terribly important. Yet another scheme to outsmart the adults, no doubt. Heaven save him from little girls.

He turned to Bethany Ross. "If you'll excuse me a moment?" he asked politely.

"Of course. I'll need a few minutes myself."

While Mitch collected Chrissie, Bethany bade the members of the school board good-night.

They met just outside the front door. He didn't have to ask where she lived—the teacher's living quarters were supplied by the state and were some of the best accommodations in town. The small two-bedroom house was located on the far side of the school gymnasium.

Mitch held open the passenger door so Chrissie could climb into the truck first. He noticed how quiet his daughter had become, as if she was in awe of this woman who would be her teacher.

"I appreciate the ride," Bethany told him once he'd started the engine.

"It's no trouble." Well, it was, but not because of the extra few minutes' driving. But then he decided he might as well let himself enjoy her company. It was a small thing and not likely to be repeated. Once the eligible men in Hard Luck caught sight of her, he wouldn't stand a chance. Which was just as well.

"Would you mind driving me around a bit?" Bethany asked. "I didn't get much of a chance to see the town when I arrived."

"There's not much to see." It occurred to him that he might enjoy her company too much, and that could be a dangerous thing.

"We could show her the library," Chrissie said eagerly.

"Hard Luck has a library?"

"It's not very big, but we use it a lot," said the girl. "Abbey's the town librarian."

Sawyer's wife had worked for weeks setting up the lending library. The books were a gift from the O'Hallorans' mother and had sat in a disorganized heap for years—until Abbey's arrival. She'd even started ordering new books, everything from best-selling fiction to cook books; the first shipment had arrived a week ago, occasioning great excitement. It seemed everyone in town had become addicted to books. Mitch often heard lively discussions revolving around a novel. An avid reader himself, he was often a patron, and he encouraged Chrissie to take out books, too.

"Ms. Ross should see the store, too," Chrissie suggested next. "And the church and the school."

"What's that building there?" Bethany asked, pointing to the largest structure in town.

"That's the lodge," he said without elaborating.

"Matt Caldwell's fixing it up." Again it was Chrissie who supplied the details. "He's Lanni's brother."

"You didn't meet Lanni Caldwell," Mitch explained. "I told you about her—she's engaged to Charles O'Halloran."

"I met Charles?"

"Briefly. He was in and out."

"The tall man wearing the Midnight Sons sweatshirt?"

"That's right."

Chrissie leaned closer to Bethany. "No one lives at the lodge now because of the fire. Matt bought it, and he's fixing it up so people will come and stay there and pay him lots of money."

"The fire?"

"It happened years ago," Mitch told her. "Most of the damage was at the back, so you can't see it from here." He shook his head. "The place should either have been repaired or torn down long before now, but I guess no one had the heart to do either. The O'Hallorans recently sold it to Matt Caldwell, which was for the best all around."

"Matt's going to take the tourists mushing!" Chrissie said, excitement raising her voice several decibels. "He's going to bring in dogs and trainers and everything!"

"That sounds like a lot of fun."

"Eagle Catcher's a husky," Chrissie added.

Mitch caught Bethany's questioning look. "That's Sawyer's dog."

"He belongs to Scott," his daughter corrected him.

"True," Mitch said with a smile at Chrissie. "I'd forgotten."

"Scott and Susan are brother and sister, right?" said Bethany. "Abbey's kids?"

"Right."

Mitch could tell Bethany was making a real effort to keep everyone straight in her mind, and he thought she'd done an impressive job so far. Maybe a memory for names and faces came with being a teacher.

"Are there any restaurants in town?" Bethany asked. "I'm not much of a cook."

Mitch glanced her way. Their eyes met briefly before he looked back at the road. "The Hard Luck Café."

Bethany smiled, amused by the name, he suspected.

"Serves the best cup of coffee in town, but then Ben hasn't got much competition."

There was a pause. "Ben?"

"Hamilton. He's an ugly cuss, but don't let that fool you. He's got a heart of gold, and he's a lot more than chief cook and bottle washer. Along with everything else, he dishes up a little psychology. You'll like him."

"I—I'm sure I will."

Mitch drove to the end of the road. A single light shone brightly in the distance. "That's where the cabins are," he explained. "Mariah's place is the one on the far left." Mitch had lost count of the number of times the youngest O'Halloran brother, Christian, had tried to convince his secretary to move into town. But Mariah always refused. Mitch was just glad *he* wasn't the one dealing with her stubbornness.

He turned the truck around and headed back toward the school. When he pulled up in front of Bethany's little house, she turned to him and smiled.

"Thanks for the tour and the ride home."

"My pleasure."

"Chrissie," Bethany said, her voice gentle, "since I'm new here, I was wondering if you'd be my helper."

His daughter's eyes lit up like sparklers on the Fourth of July, and she nodded so hard her pigtails bounced wildly. "Can Susan be your helper, too?"

"Of course."

Chrissie beamed a proud smile at her father.

"Well, good night, Chrissie, Mitch," Bethany said, then opened her door and climbed out.

"Night," father and daughter echoed. Mitch waited until she was inside the house and the lights were on before he drove off.

So, he thought *the new school teacher has arrived.*

BETHANY WAS even more tired than she'd expected. But instead of falling into a sound sleep, she lay awake, staring at the ceiling, fighting fatigue and mulling over the time she'd spent with Mitch Harris.

The man was both intense and intelligent. That much had been immediately apparent. He stood apart from the others in more ways than one. Bethany strongly suspected he wouldn't have bothered to introduce himself, which was why she'd taken the initiative. She'd noticed him right away, half-hidden in a corner, watching the events without joining in. When it looked as if the evening would pass without her meeting him, she'd made the first move.

There was something about him she found intriguing. Having lived with a policeman all her life, she must have intuitively sensed his occupation; she certainly hadn't been surprised when Sawyer told her what it was. In some remote way, he reminded her of her father. They seemed to have the same analytical mind. It drove her mother crazy, the way Dad carefully weighed each decision, considered every option, before taking action. She'd bet Mitch was the same way.

It was one personality trait Bethany *didn't* share.

She would've liked to know Mitch Harris better, but she had the distinct impression he wasn't interested. Then again...maybe he was. A breathless moment before she'd introduced herself, she'd recognized some glint of admiration in his eye. She'd been sure of it. But now she wondered if that moment had existed only in her imagination.

All the same, she couldn't help wondering what it would be like to see his eyes darken with passion just before he kissed her.

She was definitely too tired; she wasn't even thinking straight. Bethany closed her eyes and pounded the pillow, trying to force herself to relax.

But even with her eyes shut, all she saw was Mitch Harris's face.

She hadn't come to Hard Luck to fall in love, she told herself sternly.

Rolling onto her other side, she cradled the pillow in her arms. It didn't help. Drat. She could deny it till doomsday, but it wouldn't make any difference. There was just something about Chrissie's father....

"Ms. Ross?"

Bethany looked up from the back of her classroom.

Chrissie and Susan stood just inside the doorway, their faces beaming with eagerness.

"Hello, girls."

"Um, we're here to be your helpers," Chrissie said. "Dad told us we'd better make sure we *are* helpers and not nuisances."

"I'm sure you'll be wonderful helpers," Bethany said.

The two girls instantly broke into huge grins and rushed into the room. Bethany soon put them to work sorting out textbooks. This was the first time she'd taught more than one grade, and the fact that she'd now be handling kindergarten through six intimidated her more than a little.

"Everyone's looking forward to school," Chrissie announced, "especially my dad."

Bethany chuckled. Mitch wasn't so different from other parents.

The girls had been working for perhaps twenty minutes when Chrissie suddenly asked, "You're not married or anything, are you, Ms. Ross?"

A smile trembled on her mouth. "No."

"Why not?"

Leave it to a seven-year-old to ask that kind of question. "I haven't met the right man," she explained as simply as she could.

"Have you ever been in love?" Susan probed.

Bethany noticed that both girls had stopped sorting through the textbooks and were giving her their full attention. "Yes," she told them with some hesitation.

"How old are you?"

"Chrissie." Susan jabbed her elbow into her friend's ribs. "You're not supposed to ask that," she said in a loud whisper. "It's against the human-rights law. We could get charged with snooping."

"I'm twenty-five," Bethany answered, pretending she hadn't heard Susan.

The girls exchanged looks, then immediately started using their fingers to count.

"Seven," Chrissie breathed, as if it were a magic number.

"Seven?" Bethany asked curiously. What game were the girls playing?

"If a man's seven years older than you, is that too old?" Susan asked, her eyes round and inquisitive.

"Too old," Bethany repeated thoughtfully. She sat on the edge of a desk and crossed her arms. "That depends."

"On what?" Chrissie moved closer.

"On age, I suppose. If I was fourteen and wanted to date a man who was twenty-one, my parents would never have allowed it. But if I was twenty-one and he was twenty-eight, it would be okay."

Both girls looked pleased with her answer, and gave each other a high five.

Bethany decided to respond to their odd behavior with a joke. "You girls aren't thinking about dating fourteen-year-old boys, are you?" she asked, narrowing her eyes in pretend disapproval.

Chrissie covered her mouth and giggled.

Susan rolled her eyes. "Get real, Ms. Ross. I don't even know what the big attraction to boys is." Then, as if to explain her words, she added, "I have an older brother."

"Would you tell us about the man you were in love with?" This came from Chrissie. Her expression had grown so serious Bethany decided to answer, despite her initial impulse to change the subject.

"The man I was in love with," she began, "was a guy I dated while I was in college. We went out for about a year."

"What was his name?"

"Randy."

"Randy," Chrissie repeated with disgust, turning to look at her friend.

"Did he do you wrong?"

Bethany laughed, although she was uncomfortable with these questions. "No, he didn't do me wrong." If anyone was to blame for their breakup, it had been Bethany herself. She wasn't entirely sure she'd ever really loved him, which she supposed was an answer in itself. They'd been friends, and that had developed into something more—at least on Randy's part.

He'd started talking marriage and children, and at first she'd thought it sounded like a good idea. Then she'd realized she wasn't ready for that kind of commitment. Not when she had two full years of school left to complete. Not when she'd barely begun to experience life.

They'd argued and broken off their unofficial engagement. The breakup had troubled Bethany for months afterward. But now she couldn't help thinking that what she'd really regretted was the loss of the friendship.

"Do you still see him?" Chrissie asked.

Bethany nodded.

"You *do?*" Susan sounded as if this was a tragedy.

"Sometimes."

"Is he married?"

"No." Bethany grew a little sad, thinking about her longtime friend. She did miss Randy, even now, five years after their breakup.

Both Chrissie and Susan seemed deflated at the news of Bethany's lost love.

"Would it be all right if we left now?" Chrissie asked abruptly.

"That's fine," Bethany told them. "Thanks for your help."

The two disappeared so quickly all that was missing was the puff of smoke.

If nothing else, the girls certainly were entertaining, Bethany decided. She returned to the task of cutting large letters out of colored paper.

The sun blazed in through the classroom windows, and she tugged her shirt loose, unfastened the last few buttons and tied the ends at her midriff. Then she pulled her hair away from her face and used an elastic to secure it in a ponytail.

Half an hour later, most of the letters, all capitals, for the word "September" were pinned in an arch across the bulletin board at the back of the classroom. She stood on a chair and had just pinned the third *E* in place when she felt someone's presence behind her. Twisting around, she saw Mitch standing in the open door.

"Hi," she said cheerfully, undeniably pleased to see him. He was dressed in the khaki uniform worn by the Department of the Interior staff. His face revealed none of his emotions, yet Bethany had the distinct feeling he'd rather not be there.

"I'm looking for Chrissie."

Bethany pinned the *R* in place and then stepped down from the chair. "Sorry, but as you can see she isn't here."

Mitch frowned. "Louise Gold told me this was where she'd be."

Bethany remembered that Louise Gold was the woman who watched Chrissie while Mitch was at work. She'd briefly met her the day before. In addition to her other duties, Louise served on the school board.

"Chrissie was here earlier with Susan."

"I hope they behaved themselves."

Bethany recalled their probing questions and smiled to herself. Pushing the chair back into place, she said, "They were fine. I asked Chrissie for her help, remember?"

Mitch remained as far away from her as possible. Bethany suspected he'd rather track a cantankerous bear than stay in the same room with her. It was not a familiar feeling, or a pleasant one.

"She's probably over at Susan's, then," he said.

"She didn't say where she was headed."

He lingered a moment. "I don't want Chrissie to become a nuisance."

"She isn't, and neither is Susan. They're both great kids, so don't worry, okay?"

Still he hesitated. "They didn't, by chance, ask you a lot of personal questions, did they?"

"Uh...some."

He closed his eyes for a few seconds and an expression of great weariness crossed his face. He sighed. "I'll look for Chrissie over at Susan's. Thanks for your trouble."

His gaze held hers. By the time he turned away, Bethany felt a little breathless. She was certain of one thing. If it were up to Mitch Harris, she would never have left San Francisco.

Well, that was unfortunate for Mitch. Because Bethany had come to Hard Luck for a reason, and she wasn't leaving until her mission was accomplished.

Come hell or high water.

CHAPTER TWO

"DADDY?"

Mitch looked up from the Fairbanks newspaper to smile at his freckle-faced daughter. Chrissie was fresh out of the bathtub, her face scrubbed clean, her cheeks rosy. She wore her favorite *Beauty and the Beast* pajamas.

His heart clenched with the depth of the love he felt for her. No matter how miserable his marriage had been, he'd always be grateful to Lori for one thing. She'd given him Chrissie.

"It's almost bedtime," he told the seven-year-old.

"I know." Following their nightly ritual, she crawled into his lap and nestled her head against his chest. Sometimes she pretended to read the newspaper with him, but not this evening. Her thoughts seemed to be unusually grave. "Daddy, do you like Ms. Ross?"

Mitch prayed for patience. He'd been afraid of this. Chrissie had been using every opportunity to bring Bethany into the conversation, and he realized she was hoping something romantic would develop between him and the new teacher. "Ms. Ross is very nice," he answered cautiously.

"But do you *like* her?"

"I suppose."

"Do you think you'll marry her?"

It was all Mitch could do to keep from bolting out of the chair. "I have no intention of marrying anyone," he said emphatically. As far as he was concerned, the subject wasn't open to discussion. With anyone, even his daughter.

Chrissie batted her baby blues at him. "But I thought you liked her."

"Sweetheart, listen, I like Pearl, too, but that doesn't mean I'm going to marry her."

"But Pearl's old. Ms. Ross is only twenty-five. I know because I asked her. Twenty-five isn't too old, is it?"

Mitch gritted his teeth. After they'd driven Bethany home that first night, Chrissie had been filled with questions about the new teacher. No doubt she'd subjected Bethany to a similar inquisition that morning, despite his telling her not to be a nuisance.

Mitch supposed all this talk about marriage was inevitable. The summer had been full of romantic adventures. Certainly Sawyer had wasted no time in marrying Abbey; it didn't help that Abbey's daughter was Chrissie's best friend. Then Charles had become engaged to Lanni, followed by Pete and Dotty's recent announcement. To Chrissie, it must have seemed as if the whole town had caught marriage fever. Bethany, however, had been hired by the school board last spring and had nothing to do with recent influx of women to Hard Luck.

"I like Ms. Ross *so* much," Chrissie said with a delicate sigh.

"You barely know her. You might change your mind once you see her in the classroom." Mitch felt he was grasping at straws, but he was growing more and more concerned. He could hardly forbid his daughter to mention Bethany's name!

He wasn't sure what the woman had done to sprout wings and a halo in his daughter's mind. Nor did he understand why Chrissie had chosen to champion Bethany instead of, say, Mariah Douglas.

Perhaps she'd intuitively sensed his attraction to the young teacher. That idea sent chills racing down his spine. If Chrissie had figured it out, others wouldn't be far behind.

"I won't change my mind about Ms. Ross," Chrissie told him. "I think you should marry her."

"Chrissie. We've already been over this. I'm not going to marry Ms. Ross."

"Why not?"

There was something very wrong with a grown man who couldn't out-argue a seven-year-old child. "First, we don't really know each other. Remember, sweetheart, she's only been in town two days."

"But Sawyer fell in love with Abbey right away."

"Yes..." he muttered warily.

"Then I don't understand why you can't get your word in about Ms. Ross before any of the other men decide they like her, too."

"Chrissie—"

"Someone else might marry her if you don't hurry up."

Mitch calmed himself. It was clear that his daughter had an argument for every answer. "This is different," he explained reasonably. "I'm not Sawyer and Ms. Ross isn't Abbey. She came here to teach, remember? She isn't looking for a husband."

"Neither was Abbey. I really want you to marry Ms. Ross."

Mitch clenched his jaw. "I'm not marrying Ms. Ross, and I refuse to discuss it any further." He rarely used this tone with his daughter, but he wanted it understood that the conversation was over. He wasn't getting married.

End of story. No amount of begging and pleading was going to change his mind.

Chrissie was quiet for several minutes. Then she said, "Tell me about my mommy."

Mitch felt like a drowning man. Everywhere he turned there was more water, more trouble, and not a life preserver in sight. "What do you want to know?"

"Was she pretty?"

"Very pretty," he answered soothingly. Normally he found the subject of Lori painful, but right now he was grateful to discuss something other than Bethany Ross.

"As pretty as Ms. Ross?"

He rolled his eyes; he'd been sucker-punched. "Yes."

"She died in an accident?"

Mitch didn't know why Chrissie repeatedly asked the same questions about her mother. Maybe the child sensed he wasn't telling her the entire truth. "Yes, your mother died in an accident."

"And you were real sad?"

"I loved her very much."

"And she loved me?"

"Oh, yes, sweetheart, she loved you."

His daughter seemed to soak in his words, as if she needed reassurance that she'd been wanted and loved by the mother she'd never known.

After that, Chrissie grew thoughtful again. Mitch returned to his newspaper. Then, when he least expected it, she resumed her campaign. "Can I have a brother or sister someday?" she asked him. The question came at him from nowhere and scored a direct hit.

"Probably not," he told her truthfully. "I don't plan to remarry."

"Why don't you?" She wore that hurt-little-girl look that was guaranteed to weaken his resolve.

Mitch made a show of checking his wristwatch. He was through with answering questions and finding suitable arguments for a child. Through with having Bethany Ross offered up to him on a silver platter—by his daughter, the would-be matchmaker.

"It's time for bed," he said decisively.

"Already?" Chrissie whined.

"Past time." He slid her off his knee and led her into her bedroom. He removed the stuffed animals from the bed while Chrissie got down on her knees to say her prayers. She closed her eyes and folded her hands, her look intent.

Mitch could see his daughter's lips move in some fervent request. He didn't have to be a mind reader to know what she was asking. If God joined forces against him, Mitch figured he'd find himself engaged to the tantalizing Ms. Ross before the week was out.

CHRISTIAN O'HALLORAN, youngest of the three brothers, walked into the Hard Luck Café and collapsed in a chair. He propped his elbows on the tabletop and buried his face in his hands.

Without asking, Ben picked up the coffeepot and poured him a cup. "You look like you could use something stronger," he commented.

"I can't believe it," Christian muttered, running one hand down his face.

"Believe what?" Ben assumed it had something to do with Christian's secretary. He didn't understand what it was about Mariah that Christian found so objectionable. Personally he was rather fond of the young lady. Mariah Douglas had grit. She had the gumption to live in one of those rundown cabins. No power. No electric lights. And for damn sure, nothing that went flush in the night.

"You won't believe what just happened. I nearly got my head chewed off by some feminist attorney."

Now this was news. Ben slid into the chair opposite Christian's. "An attorney? Here in Hard Luck?"

Christian nodded. Even now his face remained a smoldering shade of red. "I was accused of everything from false advertising to misrepresentation and fraud. *Me*," he said incredulously.

"Who hired her?"

Christian's eyes narrowed. "My guess is Mariah."

"No." Ben found that hard to accept. Mariah might have been the cause of some minor troubles with Christian, but there wasn't a vindictive bone in her body. From everything he'd seen of her, Mariah was a sweet-natured, gentle soul.

"It isn't exactly clear who hired the woman," Christian admitted, "but odds are it's Mariah."

"I don't believe that."

"I do!" Christian snapped. "I swear to you Mariah's been looking for a way to do me in from the moment she arrived. First off, she tried to cripple me."

"She didn't mean to push that filing cabinet on your foot."

"Is that a fact? I don't suppose you noticed how perfect her aim was, did you? She's been a thorn in my side from day one. Now this."

"Seems to me you're getting sidetracked," Ben said. He didn't want to hear another litany of Mariah's supposed sins, not when there was other, juicier information to extract. "We were discussing the attorney, remember?"

Christian plowed all ten fingers though his hair. "The lawyer's name's Tracy Santiago. She flew in from some high-falutin' firm in Seattle. Let me tell you, I've seen sharks with duller teeth. This woman's after blood, and from the sound of it, she wants mine."

"And you think Mariah sent for her?" Ben asked doubtfully.

"I don't know what to think any more. Santiago's here, and when she's through discussing the details of the lawsuit with Mariah, she wants to talk to the others. To Sally McDonald and Angie Hughes." He referred to the two most recent arrivals—Sally, who worked at the town's Power and Light company, and Angie, who'd been hired as an administrative and nursing assistant to Dottie. Both of them were living in the house owned by Catherine Fletcher—Matt and Lanni Caldwell's grandmother.

"Are you going to let her?"

Christian raised his eyes until they were level with Ben's. "I can't stop her, can I? But then, I don't think a freight train would slow this Santiago woman down."

"Where is she now? At your office?" Ben asked, craning his neck to look out the window. The mobile office of Midnight Sons was parked next to the airfield, within sight of the café. He couldn't see anything out of the ordinary.

"Yeah, I had to get out of there before I said or did something I'd regret," Christian confessed. "I feel bad about abandoning Duke, but he seemed to be holding his own."

"Duke?"

"Yeah. Apparently he flew her in without knowing her purpose for coming. He made the fatal mistake of thinking she might have been another of the women I hired. Santiago let him know in no uncertain terms who and what she was. By the time they landed, the two of them were at each other's throats.''

That they'd been able to discuss anything during the flight was saying something, given how difficult it was to be heard above the roar of the engines.

''If I were this attorney,'' Christian said thoughtfully, ''I'd think twice before messing with Duke.''

Ben had to work hard to keep the smile off his face. When a feminist attorney tangled with the biggest chauvinist Ben had ever met, well...the fur was guaranteed to fly.

The door opened. Christian looked up and groaned, then covered his face with his hands.

Ben turned around and saw that it was Mariah. He lumbered to his feet, reached for the coffeepot and returned to the counter.

''Mr. O'Halloran,'' the secretary said as she timidly approached him.

''How many times,'' Christian demanded, ''have I asked you to call me by my first name? In case you haven't figured it out, there are three Mr. O'Hallorans in this town, and two of us happen to spend a good deal of time together in the same office.''

''Christian,'' she began a second time, her voice wavering slightly. ''I want you to know I had nothing to do with Ms. Santiago's arrival.''

''And pigs fly.''

Mariah clenched her hands at her sides. ''I didn't know anything about her,'' she insisted, ''and I certainly had nothing to do with hiring her.''

''Then who the hell did?''

Ben watched as Mariah closed her eyes and swallowed hard. When she spoke again, her voice was a low whisper. "I suspect it was my dad. He must have talked to her about my being here."

"And why, pray tell, would he do something like that?" Christian asked coldly.

Mariah went pale. "Would you mind very much if I sat down?"

The look Christian threw her said he would. After an awkward moment or two, he curtly gestured toward the seat across from him.

"You want any coffee?" Ben felt obliged to ask.

"No." Christian answered for her. "She doesn't want anything."

"Do you have orange juice?" Mariah asked.

"He has orange juice," Christian told her, "at five bucks a glass."

"Fine."

Another awkward moment of strained silence passed while Ben delivered the four-ounce glass of juice.

"You had something you wanted to tell me?" Christian asked impatiently.

"Yes," she said, her voice gaining strength. "I'm sure my family's responsible for Ms. Santiago's visit. You see . . . I didn't exactly tell them I'd accepted your job offer. They didn't know—"

"You mean to tell me you were in hiding from your parents?"

"I wasn't hiding," she argued. "Not exactly." She brushed the long strand of hair away from her face, and Ben noticed that her hands were shaking badly. "I wanted to prove something to them, and this seemed the only way I could do it."

"What were you trying to prove?" Christian demanded. "How easy it is to destroy a man and his business?"

"No," she replied, and squared her shoulders. "I wanted to demonstrate to my father that I'm perfectly capable of taking care of myself. That I can support myself, and furthermore, I'm old enough to make my own decisions without him continually interfering in my life."

"So you didn't tell him what you'd done."

"No," she admitted, chancing a quick look in Christian's direction. "Not at first. It's been a while since my family heard from me, so I wrote them a letter last week and told them about the job and how after a year's time I'll have the title to twenty acres and the cabin."

"And?"

"Well, with Hard Luck being in the news and everything, Dad had already heard about the deal Midnight Sons was offering women. He..." She paused and bit her lower lip. "He seems to think this isn't the place for me, and the best way to get me home is to prove you're running some kind of scam. That's why he contacted Ms. Santiago. I think he may want to sue you." She closed her eyes again, as if she expected Christian to explode.

Instead, he stared sightlessly into space. "We're dead meat," he said tonelessly. "Sawyer and I can forget everything we've ever worked for because it'll be gone."

"I explained the situation as best I could to Ms. Santiago."

"Oh, great. By now I'm sure she thinks I've kidnapped you and that I'm holding you for ransom."

"That's not true."

"Think about it, Mariah. Tracy Santiago would give her eyeteeth to cut me off at the knees—and all because you wanted to *prove something* to your father!"

"I'll take care of everything," Mariah promised. Her huge eyes implored him. "You don't have to worry. I promise I'll get everything straightened out. There won't be a lawsuit unless I'm willing to file one, and I'm not.''

''*You'll* take care of it?'' Christian repeated, and gave a short bark of laughter. ''*That's* supposed to reassure me? Ha!''

LANNI CALDWELL glanced at her watch for the third time in a minute. Charles was late. He'd promised to pick her up in front of the *Anchorage News,* where she was working as an intern. She should wait outside for him he'd said. It had been ten days since they'd last seen each other, and she'd never missed anyone so much.

They'd agreed to postpone their wedding until the first week of April. At the time, that hadn't sounded so terrible, but she'd since revised her opinion. If these ten days were any indication of how miserable she was going to be without him, she'd never last the eight months. Her one consolation was that his travel schedule often brought him to Valdez, which was only a short airplane trip from Anchorage.

Just when she was beginning to really worry, Lanni saw him. He was smiling broadly, a smile that spoke of his own joy at seeing her.

Unable to stand still, Lanni hurried toward him, threading her way through the late-afternoon shoppers crowding the sidewalks.

When she was only a few feet away, she started to run. ''Charles! Oh, Charles!''

He caught her around the waist and lifted her off the ground. They were both talking at once, saying the same things. How lonely the past days had been. How eight months seemed impossible. How much they'd missed each other. She stopped, simply because there wasn't enough air in her lungs to continue.

It felt so incredibly good to be in his arms again. She hadn't *intended* to kiss him right there on the sidewalk with half of Anchorage looking on, but she couldn't stop herself. Charles O'Halloran was solid and handsome and strong—and he was hers.

His mouth found Lanni's and her objections, her doubts, her misery all melted away. She hardly heard the traffic sounds, hardly noticed the smiling passersby.

Slowly Charles lowered her to the ground. He dragged in a giant breath; so did she. "When it comes to you, Lanni," he whispered, "I haven't got a bit of self-control."

They clasped hands and started walking. "Where are we going?" she asked.

"We have to go somewhere?" he teased.

Lanni leaned her head against his shoulder. "No, but dinner would be nice. I'm starved."

"Me, too, but I'm even more starved for you."

Lanni smiled softly. "I'm dying to hear what came of the lawyer's visit to Hard Luck. What's this about Mariah being the one who's filing the lawsuit? I don't know her well, but I can't see her doing that."

"I'll explain everything later," he promised, wrapping his arm around her, keeping her close to his side.

"All I can say is that Christian deserves whatever he gets. He's been so impatient with her."

Charles's eyes met Lanni's, then crinkled in silent amusement. "Just whose side are you on in this fiasco?"

"Yours," she said promptly. "It's just that I find it all rather...entertaining."

"Is that a fact?" He brought her hand to his lips and kissed her knuckles. "Christian's convinced we're in a damned-if-we-do and damned-if-we-don't situation."

"Really?" Her eyes held his. This could well be more serious than it sounded. "Is Midnight Sons in legal trouble?"

Charles held open the door of her favorite Chinese restaurant. "I don't know. Frankly it's not my problem. Sawyer and Christian are the ones who came up with this brilliant plan to bring women to Hard Luck. I'm sure that between them they'll find a solution."

They were promptly seated and the waiter took their order. "Don't look so worried," Charles said, gripping her hand across the table. "As far as I'm concerned, this is a tempest in a teacup. Mariah's parents are the ones who started this, so I suggested we let Mariah work this out with them. Her father doesn't want to ruin Midnight Sons; all he really cares about is making sure his daughter's safe and sound."

"I'd say Mariah can look after herself very well indeed. She's bright and responsible and—"

"Christian might not agree with you, but I do."

A smile stole across Lanni's features. "You're going to make me a very good husband, Charles O'Halloran."

For long moments they simply gazed at each other. To Lanni there was no better man than Charles, and her heart swelled with love and pride. Of all the women in the world, he'd chosen to marry *her*—but then, she was convinced their falling in love had been no accident.

"I talked to your mother," she said, suddenly remembering the lengthy conversation she'd had earlier with Ellen Greenleaf. Ellen had remarried a couple of years ago and was now living in British Columbia.

"And?"

"And she's absolutely delighted that you came to your senses and proposed."

"I proposed?" he chided. "It seems to me it was the other way around."

"Does it really matter who asked whom?" she said in mock disgust. "The important thing is I love you and you love me."

Charles grew serious. "I do love you."

Lanni would never doubt him. Slowly he raised her hand to his lips and kissed her palm. The action was both sensual and endearing.

"Does your grandmother know about us?" Charles asked.

Lanni shook her head. "Her health has deteriorated in the last couple of weeks. Mom said Grammy doesn't even know who she is half the time. Apparently she slips in and out of consciousness. The doctors...don't expect her to live much longer."

Charles frowned and his eyes grew sad. "I'm sorry, Lanni."

"I know you are."

"I spent a lot of years hating Catherine Fletcher for what she did to my family, but I can't any longer. It's because of her that I found the most precious gift of my life. You. Remember what you said a few weeks ago about the two of us being destined for each other? I believe it now as strongly as I believe anything."

BETHANY HAD PURPOSELY waited three days before making her way to the Hard Luck Café. She'd needed the time to fortify herself for this first confrontation. The night of her arrival, Mitch had confirmed what she already knew: Ben Hamilton owned the café.

Her heart scampered, then thudded so hard it was almost painful. Her palms felt sweaty as she pulled open the door and stepped inside. If she reacted this way before she even met Ben, what would she be like afterward?

"Hello."

Ben stood behind the counter, a white apron wrapped around his middle, a welcoming smile on his lips. Bethany felt as if the wind had been knocked out of her.

"You must be Bethany Ross."

"Yes," she said, struggling to make her voice audible. "You're Ben Hamilton?"

"The one and only." He sketched a little bow, then leaned back against the counter, studying her.

With her breath trapped in her lungs, Bethany made a show of glancing around the empty room. It was eleven-thirty, still early for lunch. The café sported a counter and a number of booths with red vinyl upholstery. The rest of the furnishings consisted of tables and mismatched chairs.

"Help yourself to a seat."

"Thank you." Bethany chose to sit at the counter. She reached for a plastic-coated menu and pretended to study it.

"The special of the day is a roast-beef sandwich," Ben told her.

She looked up and nodded. "What about the soup?"

"Split pea."

Ben was nothing like she'd expected. The years hadn't been as generous to him as she'd hoped. His hair had thinned and his belly hung over the waistband of his apron. Lines creased his face.

If he hadn't introduced himself, hadn't said his name aloud, Bethany never would have guessed.

"Do you want any recommendations?" he asked.

"Please."

"Go with the special."

She closed the menu. "All right, I will."

As he walked back into the kitchen, he asked, "How are things going for you at the school?"

"Fine," she said, surprised she was able to carry on a normal conversation with him. "The kids are great, and Margaret's been a lot of help."

She wondered what Ben saw when he looked at her. Did he notice any resemblance? Did he see how much she looked like her mother, especially around the eyes? Or had he wiped the memory of her mother from his mind?

"Everyone in Hard Luck's real pleased to have you."

"I'm pleased to be here," she answered politely. She was struck by how friendly and helpful he was, how genuinely interested he seemed. Was it because of that quality her mother had fallen in love with him all those years ago?

The door opened and Ben looked up. "Howdy, Mitch. Said hello to the new schoolteacher yet?"

"We met earlier." Bethany thought she detected a note of reluctance in his voice, as if he regretted coming into the café while she was there.

Mitch claimed the stool at the opposite end of the counter.

"I don't think she's contagious," Ben chided from the kitchen, and chuckled. "And she doesn't look like she bites."

Mitch cast Bethany an apologetic glance. Uncomfortable, she glanced away.

Ben brought her meal, and she managed to meet his eyes. "I . . . I meant to tell you I wanted to take the sandwich with me," she said, faltering over the words. "If that would be all right."

"No problem." He whipped the plate off the counter. "What can I get for you, Mitch?" he asked.

"How about a cheeseburger?"

"You got it." Ben returned to the kitchen, leaving Bethany and Mitch alone.

She looked at him. He looked at her. Neither seemed able to come up with anything to say. In other circumstances, Bethany would have found a hundred different subjects to discuss.

But not now. Not when she was so distracted by the battle being waged in her heart. She'd just walked up to her father and ordered lunch.

No, he *wasn't* her father, she amended. Her father was Peter Ross, the man who'd loved her and raised her as his own. The man who'd sat at her bedside and read her to sleep. The man who'd escorted her to the father-daughter dance when she was a high school sophomore.

The only link Bethany shared with Ben Hamilton was genetic. He was the man who'd given her life, and nothing else. Not one damn thing.

CHAPTER THREE

ON THE FIRST DAY of school, Mitch swore his daughter was up before dawn. By the time the alarm sounded and he struggled out of bed and into the kitchen, Chrissie was already dressed.

She sat in the living room with her lunch pail tightly clutched in her hand. She was dressed in her flashy new jeans and Precious Moments sweatshirt.

"Morning, Daddy."

"Howdy, pumpkin." He yawned loudly. "Aren't you up a little early?" He padded barefoot into the kitchen, with Chrissie following him.

"It's the first day of school." She announced this as if it was news to him.

"I know."

"Ms. Ross said I could be her helper again."

Mitch had stopped counting the number of times a day Chrissie mentioned Ms. Ross. He'd given up telling her he wasn't interested in marrying the teacher. Chrissie didn't want to believe him, and arguing with her only irritated him. In time, she'd see for herself that there would never be a relationship between him and Bethany.

He'd heard that Bethany had stirred up a lot of interest among the single men in town. Good. Great. Wonderful. Soon enough, she'd be involved with someone else, and his daughter would get the message.

Mitch hated to disappoint his tenderhearted seven-year-old. But, he reasoned, disappointment was a part of life, and he wouldn't always be able to protect her. The sooner she accepted there would be only the two of them, the better.

"I packed my own lunch," she told him proudly, holding up her Barbie lunch pail.

"I'm proud of you."

She delighted in showing him what she'd chosen for her lunch. Ham-and-cheese sandwich carefully wrapped in napkins, an apple, juice, an oatmeal cookie. Mitch was pleased to see that she'd done a good job of packing a well-balanced meal and told her so.

He looked at his watch, gauging the time before they could leave. "What about breakfast?"

Although Chrissie claimed she was too excited to eat anything, Mitch insisted she try. "How about a bowl of cereal?" he suggested, pulling out several boxes from the cupboard. He wasn't much of a breakfast eater himself. Generally he didn't have anything until ten or so. More often than not, he picked up a doughnut or something equally sweet when he stopped in for coffee at Ben's.

"I'll *try* to eat something," Chrissie agreed with a decided lack of enthusiasm. He let her pour her own cereal and milk. His daughter was an independent little creature, which was fine with Mitch. He took pride in the fact that Chrissie could take care of herself.

By the time he'd finished dressing, she'd eaten her breakfast and washed and put away her bowl and spoon. She sat on the couch waiting for Mitch to escort her to school.

"Are you sure you need me, now that you're a second-grader?" Not that Mitch objected to walking his daughter to class. However, he had a sneaking suspicion that if the teacher had been anyone other than the lovely Ms. Ross, Chrissie would have insisted on walking without him.

"I *want* you to take me," she said with a smile bright enough to blind him. The kid knew exactly what she was doing. And being the good father he was, he had to go along with her. The way he figured it, he'd walk her to the school door and, if he was lucky, escape without seeing Bethany.

His plan backfired. Chrissie insisted on showing him her desk.

"I'm over here," she said, taking him by the hand and leading him to the front row. "Ms. Ross let me pick my own seat." Wouldn't you know, his daughter had chosen to sit directly in front of the teacher's desk.

He tried to make a fast getaway, but Bethany herself waylaid him.

"Good morning, Mitch."

"Morning." The tropical bird was back in full plumage. She wore a hot pink skirt with a colorful floral top; it reminded him of the shirt Sawyer had brought back from Hawaii. Her hair was woven into a thick braid that fell halfway down her back.

She did have beautiful hair, he'd say that much. It didn't take a lot of effort to imagine undoing her braid and running his fingers through the glossy strands. He could see himself with his hands buried wrist-deep in her hair, drawing her mouth to his. Her lips would feel silky soft, and she'd taste like honey and passion and—

"Are you picking me up after school?" Chrissie asked, interrupting his thoughts.

Thank heavens she had. Apparently all Chrissie's chatter about Bethany was having more of an effect on him than he'd realized. His heart pounded like an overworked piston, his pulse thumping so hard he could feel it throb in his neck.

Bethany and Chrissie were both looking at him, awaiting his response. "Pick you up?" As a rule, Chrissie walked over to Louise Gold's house after school.

"Just for today," Chrissie said, her big eyes gazing up at him hopefully.

"All right," he agreed grudgingly. "Just for today."

Chrissie's face shone with her smile.

He would've bidden Bethany farewell, but she was talking to other parents. Just as well. The sooner he got away from her, the sooner he could get a grip on his emotions.

Mitch wished to hell he knew what was wrong with him. After vehemently opposing all talk about becoming romantically involved, he found it downright frightening to discover the overwhelming effect she had on him. There was only one way he could account for it.

He'd been too long without a woman.

SAWYER DEBATED what exactly he should say to his brother. It wasn't often he felt called upon to take Christian to task. But enough was enough. Christian had Mariah so unnerved the poor girl couldn't do anything right.

"She did it again," Christian muttered as he walked past Sawyer's desk to his own.

Sawyer looked up. "Who?" he asked in an innocent voice.

Seething, Christian jerked his head toward Mariah. "She can't seem to find accounts receivable on the computer."

"It's here," Mariah insisted, her fingers on the keyboard. Even from where Sawyer was sitting, it looked as though she was randomly pressing keys in a desperate effort to find the missing data. "I'm just not sure where it went."

"Don't you have it on a backup disk?" Sawyer asked.

"Yes . . ."

"Who knows?" Christian tossed his hands in the air. "The backup disk might well be the same place as the missing file. We could be in real trouble here." Panic edged his voice.

"She'll find it," Sawyer said confidently.

Mariah thanked him with a brief smile.

"Let me look," Christian demanded, flying out of his chair. "Before you do something more serious and crash the entire system."

"I lost it, I'll find it." Mariah didn't budge from her seat. The woman had long since won Sawyer's admiration, not least for the mettle she'd shown in dealing with his brother.

"Leave her be," Sawyer said.

"And risk everything?"

"We aren't risking anything. There's a backup disk."

Christian sat down at his desk, but his gaze remained glued on Mariah. Sawyer watched Christian. And Mariah did her level best to ignore them both.

"Fact is, I could use a break," Sawyer said. "Why don't we let Ben treat us to a cup of his coffee?"

"All right," Christian agreed reluctantly.

As Sawyer walked past Mariah's desk, she mouthed a thank-you. He nodded and steered his irritable brother out the door.

"I wish you wouldn't be so hard on her," he said the minute they were alone. It annoyed him to see Christian treat Mariah as if she didn't have a brain in her head.

"Hard on her?" Christian protested loudly. "The woman drives me insane. If it was up to me, she'd be out of here in a heartbeat. She's trouble with a capital *T.* "

"She's a damn good secretary," Sawyer argued. "The office has never been in better shape. The files are organized and neat, and the equipment's been updated. Frankly I can't believe we managed without a secretary as long as we did."

Christian opened his mouth, then closed it. He didn't have an argument.

"Okay, so there was the one fiasco with that attorney," Sawyer said, knowing that part of Christian's anger stemmed from the confrontation with Tracy Santiago.

Christian's mouth thinned and his eyes narrowed. "Mark my words, she'll be back."

"Who?"

His brother eyed him as if he was dense. "The attorney. If for nothing more than pure spite. That woman's vicious, Sawyer. Vicious. And as if that's not bad enough, she took an instant dislike to all of us—especially Duke. She's out for revenge."

Sawyer didn't believe that. True, Christian had been the one who'd actually talked to her, but his brother's assessment of Tracy's plans for revenge sounded a little farfetched.

"It's my understanding that everything was squared once Mariah talked to her. I don't think there's any real threat."

"For now, you mean," Christian said meaningfully. "But don't think we've heard the end of this. Yup, you mark my words, Santiago's gone for reinforcements."

"Don't be ridiculous. Why would she do that if no one is paying her fee? We've seen the last of her."

"I doubt it," Christian muttered.

Instead of heading straight to Ben's, they strolled toward the open hangar. John Henderson, who served as a sometime mechanic and a full-time pilot, was servicing the six-passenger Lockheed, the largest plane in their small fleet.

When he saw them approach, John grabbed an oil rag from his hip pocket and wiped his hands. "Morning," he called out cheerfully.

Sawyer noticed that John had gotten his hair and beard trimmed. He wasn't a bad-looking guy when he put some effort into his appearance. Of course, there hadn't been much reason to do that until recently.

It occurred to him that Duke Porter might learn a thing or two from John. Duke might have fared better with the Santiago woman had he been a bit more gentlemanly. Sawyer had never seen any two people take such an instant dislike to one another.

"You're looking dapper," he commented, nodding at John, and to his surprise, the other man blushed.

"I was thinking of asking the new schoolteacher if she'd have dinner with me Friday evening," he said. Sawyer noted that John was looking at Christian as if he expected him to object.

"It's Thursday, John," Sawyer pointed out. "Just when do you plan to ask her?"

"That depends." Again John studied Christian.

"What are you looking at me for?" Christian snapped, his mood as surly with John as it had been earlier with Mariah.

"I just wanted to be sure you weren't planning on asking her yourself."

"Why would I do that?" The glance Christian gave Sawyer said he had more than enough problems with *one* woman.

John's face broke into a wide grin of unspoken relief. "That's great."

Christian grumbled something under his breath as he headed out the other side of the hangar. Sawyer followed him to the Hard Luck Café.

As they sat down at the counter, Ben stuck his head out from the kitchen. "It's self-service this morning, fellows."

"No problem." Sawyer walked around the counter and reached for the pot. He filled two mugs. Meanwhile, Christian helped himself to a couple of powdered-sugar doughnuts from under the plastic dome.

"Getting back to Mariah," Sawyer said when he'd finished stirring his coffee. He felt obliged to clear this up; in his opinion, Christian's attitude needed a bit of adjusting.

"Do we have to?"

"Yes, we do. She's proved herself a capable secretary."

"The woman's nothing but a nuisance. She can't type worth a damn, she misfiles correspondence, and she habitually loses things. The accounts-receivable disaster this morning is a prime example."

"I've never had any trouble with her," Sawyer countered. "I've found Mariah to be hardworking and sincere."

"She makes too many mistakes."

"Frankly I don't see it. If you ask me, *you're* the problem. You make her nervous. She's constantly worried that she's going to mess up—it's a self-fulfilling prophecy. Besides," Sawyer added, "she's gone to a lot of trouble to work things out with her family and settle this lawsuit business. I admire her for that."

Apparently Christian didn't share his admiration. "I wish they'd talked her into heading back to Seattle. It's where she belongs."

Sawyer merely shrugged. "Face the fact that Mariah's going to stay the entire year. It's a matter of pride with her, and that's something we can both appreciate."

Christian looked away.

"She isn't so bad, you know." Sawyer slapped his brother affectionately on the back. "There's one other thing you seem to have conveniently forgotten."

"What's that?"

Sawyer snagged one of Christian's doughnuts. He grinned broadly. "You must have liked *something* about her. After all, you're the one who hired her."

"In other words, I don't have anyone to blame but myself."

"You got it." With that Sawyer walked out of the café, leaving his brother to foot the bill.

IN TWO WEEKS Bethany hadn't seen even a glimpse of Mitch Harris. The man made himself as scarce as sunlight in an Alaskan winter. He must be working overtime, and she had to wonder if it was—at least partly—in an effort to avoid her.

Bethany could accept that he wasn't attracted to her if indeed that was the case. But the night they'd met and each time afterward, she'd sensed a growing awareness between them. She knew he felt it, too, even though he doggedly resisted it. Whenever they were in a room together, no matter how many other people were present, their eyes gravitated toward each other. The solid ground beneath Bethany would subtly shift, and she'd have to struggle to hide the fact that anything was wrong.

"Can I clean the blackboards for you, Ms. Ross?" Chrissie asked, interrupting her musings. The youngster stood next to Bethany's desk. It would be very easy to love this child, she thought.

Chrissie had been her student for two weeks, and it became increasingly difficult not to make her a teacher's pet. The seven-year-old was so willing to please and always looked for ways to brighten Bethany's day.

If Bethany had any complaints about Mitch's daughter, it was the number of times Chrissie introduced her father into the conversation. Clearly the girl adored him.

"Can I?" she asked again, holding up the erasers.

"Certainly, Chrissie. What a thoughtful thing to ask. I'd be delighted if you cleaned the blackboards."

Chrissie flushed with pleasure. "I like to help my dad, too. He needs me sometimes."

"I'll bet you're good at helping him. You've been a wonderful assistant to me."

Once more the child glowed at Bethany's approval. "My dad promised to pick me up after school today," she said; she seemed to be watching for Bethany's reaction to that news. From other bits of information Chrissie had dropped, Bethany knew that Mitch occasionally came for his daughter after school. She herself hadn't seen him.

"With your dad coming, maybe you should skip cleaning the boards this afternoon," Bethany said. She didn't want Mitch to be kept waiting because Chrissie was busy, nor did she want to force him to enter the classroom.

"It'll be all right," Chrissie said quickly. "Don't worry, Dad'll wait."

Still, Bethany wasn't really confident she was doing the right thing, especially since Mitch seemed to be avoiding her so diligently.

The little girl was busy with the blackboards, standing on tiptoes to reach as far as she could, when Mitch walked briskly into the classroom. His movements were filled with impatience. His body language said he didn't appreciate having to come look for his daughter.

As had happened before, his eyes flew to Bethany's, and hers to his. Slowly she rose from behind her desk. "Hello, Mitch."

"Bethany."

"Hi, Dad. I'm helping Ms. Ross. I'm almost done," Chrissie said lightheartedly. "All I have to do is go outside and stamp the chalk out of the erasers. I promise I'll only take a minute."

Mitch opened his mouth as though to protest, but before he could utter a word, Chrissie raced out the door.

Bethany and Mitch were alone.

They couldn't stop staring at each other. Bethany would have paid good money to know what he was thinking. Not that she was all that clear about her own feelings. Their attraction to each other *should* have been uncomplicated. It wasn't as though either of them was involved with anyone else.

True, John Henderson, one of the bush pilots employed by Midnight Sons, had asked her to dinner. She'd accepted; there was no point in sitting around waiting for Mitch to ask her out, and John seemed pleasant.

The silence between them grew louder. Mitch's face was stern, his features set. Bethany sighed, uncertain how to break the ice.

"I understand you're going out to dinner with John Henderson this evening," Mitch surprised her by mentioning.

"Yes." She wasn't going to deny it.

"I think that's a good idea."

"My having dinner with John?"

"Yes."

Their eyes remained locked. Finally she swallowed and asked, "Why?"

"John's a good man."

It was on the tip of her tongue to ask the reason Mitch hadn't asked her out himself. Mitch was attracted to her, and she to him. The force of that attraction was no small thing. Surely it would be better to discuss it openly, even if they didn't act on their feelings. She longed to toss out the subject and see where it would take them. But in the end she said nothing. Neither did Mitch.

Chrissie reentered the classroom, and Bethany slowly moved her gaze from Mitch to his daughter.

"The erasers are clean," Chrissie announced. Her eyes were filled with expectation.

"Thank you, sweetheart."

"You're welcome. Can I clean them again next Friday?"

"That would be very thoughtful."

"Have a nice evening," Mitch said as he walked out the door, his hand on his daughter's shoulder.

"I will, thank you," she called after them, but she didn't think Mitch heard.

The encounter with Mitch left Bethany feeling melancholy. She accompanied Margaret Simpson to her house for a cup of coffee, hoping that a visit with the other teacher would cheer her up; however, despite herself, she remained distracted during their conversation. Once she arrived home, she turned on her CD player and lay down on the carpet in the living room, listening to Billy Joel— which said a good deal about her state of mind.

Instead of being excited about her dinner date, she was bemoaning the fact that it wasn't Mitch taking her out. It was time to face reality: he wasn't interested in seeing her. She told herself it didn't matter. It wasn't the end of the world. There were plenty of other fish in the sea. But her little pep talk fell decidedly flat.

Because John was afraid he might get back late from a flight into Fairbanks, he'd asked if they could meet at the Hard Luck Café. Bethany didn't object. She showered and changed into a knee-length, chocolate brown skirt, an extra-long, loose-knit beige sweater and calf-length leather boots. To dress up the outfit, she wove a silk scarf into her French braid. She looked good and knew it. Her one regret was that Mitch wouldn't see her. She'd like him to know what he was missing!

To her surprise, there were only two other people in the café when she arrived. The men, deeply engrossed in conversation, sat drinking beer at one of the tables.

"My, my, don't you look pretty," Ben hailed her when she took a seat in a booth near the window. Apparently he knew she was meeting John, because he filled two water glasses and tucked a couple of menus under his arm.

"Thank you."

"I heard John's got his eye on you."

Bethany didn't comment. Although she'd been into the café a number of times since her arrival, she was never completely comfortable with Ben. She'd moved to Hard Luck with an open mind about him. She had no plan other than getting to know this man who'd fathered her.

It was something she'd learned only a year ago. Despite the initial shock, this new knowledge didn't change her feelings toward either her mother or Peter Ross. She just wanted to discover for herself what kind of man Ben Hamilton was. She certainly didn't intend to interfere in his life. Nor did she intend to embarrass him with the truth. The year might well come to a close without his ever knowing who she was.

In all honesty, Bethany couldn't think of a way to casually announce that she was his daughter. For a giddy moment, she was tempted to throw open her arms and call him Daddy. But, no—he'd never been that.

Ben lingered at the table. "If you want the truth, I was surprised you were coming here with John."

"Really." Bethany picked up the water glass.

"I kinda thought you were sweet on Mitch."

The glass hit the table with an unexpected thunk, garnering the attention of the restaurant's two other occupants.

Ben rubbed the side of his face. "What I've seen, Mitch is taken with you, as well."

Bethany gazed down at the table and swallowed nervously. "I'm sure that isn't true."

Low laughter rumbled in Ben's chest. "I've seen the way you two send looks at each other. I'm not blind, you know. Yes, sir, I see plenty—lots more than people think." He tapped his finger on his temple to emphasize the point. "I might be a crusty old bachelor, but I—"

"You never married?" she interrupted him.

"No."

"Why not?" She turned the conversation away from herself, at the same time attempting to learn what she could of his life.

"I guess you could say I never found the right woman."

His answer irritated Bethany. Her mother was one of the finest women she'd ever known. The desire to defend her mother, tell this character about the heartache he'd caused, burned in the pit of her stomach.

"How...how long have you been in Alaska?" she asked, instead.

Ben seemed to need time to calculate his answer. "It must be twenty years now. The O'Halloran boys were still wet behind the ears when I made my way here."

"Why Hard Luck?" she asked.

"Why not? It was as good a place as any. Besides," he said, flashing her a grin, "there's something to be said for having the only restaurant within a four-hundred-mile radius."

Bethany laughed.

The door opened and John Henderson rushed in, a little breathless and a whole lot flustered. He hurried over to the table, and his eyes lit up at the sight of her. He seemed speechless.

"Hello again," Bethany said.

John remained standing there, his mouth open.

Ben slapped him on the back. "Aren't you going to thank me for keeping her company?"

John jerked his head around as if noticing Ben for the first time. "Thanks, Ben."

"No trouble." He turned to walk back to the kitchen, but before he did, Bethany's eye caught his and they shared a secret smile. It was a small thing, this smile, but for the first time Bethany felt as if she'd truly communicated with the man she'd come three thousand miles to meet.

DINNER TURNED OUT to be more of an ordeal than Bethany had expected. By the time he'd paid for their meal, Bethany actually felt sorry for John. During the course of their dinner, he'd dripped gravy down the front of his shirt, overturned the sugar canister and spilled his cup of coffee, half of which landed on her skirt. The man was clearly a nervous wreck.

"I'll walk you home," John said.

She waited until they were outside before she thanked him. Although it was only two weeks into September, there was a decided coolness, and the hint of snow hung in the air. Bethany was glad she'd worn her coat.

"Thank you, John, for a lovely evening."

The pilot buried his hands in his jacket pockets. "I'm sorry about the coffee."

"You didn't do it on purpose."

"What about your skirt?"

"Don't worry—I'm sure it'll wash out."

"You didn't get burned?"

She'd assured him she hadn't at least a dozen times. "I'm fine, John, really."

"I want you to know I'm not normally this clumsy."

"I'm sure that's true."

"It's just that it isn't often a woman as beautiful as you agrees to have dinner with me."

There was something touching about this pilot, something endearing. "What a sweet thing to say. Thank you."

"Women like to hear that kind of stuff, don't they?" John asked. "About being pretty and all."

Bethany hesitated, wondering where the conversation was heading. "I'd say it was safe to say we do."

It was difficult to keep from smiling. With someone else, she might have been irritated or worse. But not with

John. Besides, the evening was so beautiful. The sky danced with a brilliant display of stars, and the northern lights seemed to sizzle just over the horizon. Bethany couldn't stop gazing up at the heavens.

"Is it always this beautiful here?"

"Yup," John said without hesitation. "But then they say that beauty's in the eye of the beholder."

"That's true," Bethany admitted, a little puzzled.

"It won't be long now before the rivers freeze," he explained soberly.

"So soon?"

"Yup. We're likely to have snow anytime."

Bethany could hardly believe it. "Really?"

"This is the Arctic, Bethany."

"But it seems as if I just got here. It's still summer at home."

"Maybe in California it is, but not here." He looked worried. "You aren't going to leave, are you?"

"No. I signed a contract for this school year. Don't worry, I'm not going to break my commitment because of a little snow and ice."

They strolled past the school, and she glanced at the building with a sense of pride. She loved her job and her students.

Soon her house was within sight. Bethany was deciding how to handle the awkwardness that might develop when they reached her front door. She didn't plan to invite John in.

"Thank you," Bethany said again when at last they stood on the stoop.

"The evening would've been better if I hadn't . . . you know."

"Stop worrying about a little coffee."

"Don't forget the sugar canister." He grinned as if he'd begun to find the entire episode amusing.

"Despite a few, uh, mishaps, I really did enjoy dinner," she told him.

John kicked at the dirt with the toe of his shoe. "I don't suppose you'd consider going out with me again."

Bethany wasn't sure how to respond. She liked John, but only as a friend, and she didn't want to mislead him into thinking something more could develop between them. She'd made that mistake once before.

"You don't need to feel guilty if you don't want to," he said, his eyes avoiding hers. He cleared his throat. "I can understand why someone hand-delivered by the angels wouldn't want to be seen with someone like me." He glanced shyly at her.

"How about if we have dinner again next Friday night?" she asked.

John's head shot up. "You mean it?"

Bethany smiled. "This time it'll be my treat."

His smile faded and he crossed his arms on his chest. "You want to buy *me* dinner?"

"Yes. Friends do that, you know." A car could be heard in the distance slowly making its way down the street.

"Friends, you say?" The car was coming closer.

She nodded and leaned forward and very gently pressed her lips to his cheek. As she backed away, she noticed the car had stopped.

Silhouetted against the moonlight sat Mitch Harris. He'd just witnessed her kissing John Henderson.

CHAPTER FOUR

THE FIRST SNOWFALL of the year arrived in the third week of September. Thick flurries drifted down throughout the day, covering the ground and obscuring familiar outlines. Mitch thought he should have been accustomed to winter's debut by now, but he wasn't. However beautiful, however serene, this soft-looking white blanket was only a foretaste of the bitter cold to follow.

He looked at his watch. In a few minutes he'd walk over to the school to meet Chrissie. He'd gotten into the habit of picking his daughter up on Friday afternoons.

Not because she needed him or had asked him to come. No, he wryly suspected that going to the school was rooted in some masochistic need to see Bethany.

He rationalized that he was giving Chrissie this extra attention because he worked longer hours on Friday evenings, when Diane Hestead, a high school student, stayed with her. That was the only night of the week Ben served alcohol. Before the women had arrived, a few of the pilots and maybe a trapper or two wandered into the Hard Luck Café. But with the news of women coming to town, Ben's place had begun to fill up, not only with pilots but pipeline workers and other men.

For the past three Friday nights, John Henderson and

Bethany had dined at the café. They came and left before eight, when Ben opened the bar.

From the gossip circulating around town, Mitch learned that they'd become something of an item, although both insisted they were "only friends."

Mitch knew otherwise. On Bethany's first date with John, he'd happened upon them kissing. Friends indeed! Even now, his gut tightened at the memory.

For the thousandth time he reminded himself that he'd been the one to encourage her to see John. He couldn't very well reveal his discontent with that situation when she'd done nothing more than follow his advice.

He'd tried to convince himself that his discovering John and Bethany together—kissing—had been sheer coincidence. But it hadn't been.

As the public-safety officer, Mitch routinely checked the streets on Friday nights. He'd seen the two leave Ben's place on foot that first evening and had discreetly followed them. On subsequent Fridays he'd continued his spy tactics, always making sure he was out of sight. He wasn't particularly proud of himself, but he found it impossible to resist the compulsion.

Except for their first date, when he'd seen them kissing outside her house, she'd invited John in. The pilot never stayed more than a few minutes, but of course Mitch knew what the two of them were doing.

He kept telling himself he should be pleased she was dating John; Henderson was a decent sort. But Mitch *wasn't* pleased. At nights he lay awake staring at the four shrinking walls of his bedroom. Still, he knew it wasn't the walls that locked him in, that kept him from building a relationship with Bethany.

It was his guilt, his own doubts and fears, that came between him and Bethany. This was Lori's legacy to him.

She'd died and in that moment made certain he'd never be free of her memory.

Mitch checked his watch a second time and decided to head over to the school. The phone rang as he closed and locked the door, but he resisted the temptation to answer it. The machine would pick up the message, and he'd deal with the call when he returned to the office.

Mitch could hear excited laughter in the distance as the children frolicked in the snow. Chrissie loved playing outside, although there would be precious little of that over the next few months.

By the time Christmas came, Hard Luck would be in total darkness. But with the holidays to occupy people's minds and lift their spirits, the dark days didn't seem nearly as depressing as they might have.

Mitch had just rounded the corner to the school when he saw Bethany. She half trotted with her head bowed against the wind, her steps filled with frantic purpose. She glanced up and saw him and stopped abruptly.

"Mitch." Her hand pushed a stray lock of hair away from her face, and he noticed for the first time how pale she was. "It's Chrissie. She's been hurt."

The words hit Mitch like a fist. He ran toward her and gripped her by the elbows. *"What happened?"*

"She fell on the ice and cut herself. The school tried to phone you, but you'd already left the office."

"Where is she?"

"At the Clinic..." Bethany's voice quavered precariously. "I knew you were probably on your way to the school. Oh, Mitch, I'm so afraid."

It was bad. It had to be, otherwise Bethany wouldn't be this pale, this frightened. Panic galvanized him and he began running toward the clinic. He'd gone half a block before he realized that Bethany was behind him, her untutored feet slipping and sliding on the snow. Fearing she might stumble and fall, he turned back and stretched out a hand to her. She grasped his fingers with surprising strength.

Together they hurried toward the clinic. It couldn't have taken them more than two or three minutes to reach the building, but it felt like a lifetime to Mitch. He couldn't bear the thought of something happening to Chrissie. His daughter, his joy. It was she who'd given his life purpose following Lori's death, she who'd given him a reason for living.

He jerked open the clinic door, and the first thing he saw was blood. Crimson droplets on the floor. Chrissie's blood. He stopped cold as icy fingers crept along his backbone.

Dotty Harlow, the nurse who'd replaced Pearl Inman, was nowhere in sight; neither was Angie Hughes.

"Dotty!" he called urgently.

"Daddy." Chrissie moaned his name, and the sound of her pain cut at his heart.

Dotty stepped out of a cubicle in the back. Her soothing voice calmed his panic as she explained that Chrissie required a couple of stitches, which she was qualified to do.

Angie, who'd been talking to Chrissie, stepped aside when he came into the room. Chrissie sniffled loudly and her small arms circled his neck; when she spoke, her words came in a staccato hiccupping voice. "I... fell... and cut my leg real... bad."

"You're going to be fine, pumpkin." Gently he pressed his hand to the side of her sweet face and laid his cheek on her hair.

"I want Ms. Ross."

"I'm here," Bethany whispered from behind Mitch.

Chrissie stretched out her arms and Bethany hugged her close. Watching the two of them together threatened his resolve, as nothing else could have, to guard his heart against this woman.

"You were very brave," Dotty told Chrissie, as she put away the medical supplies.

"I tried not to cry," Chrissie said, tears glistening in her eyes, "but it hurt too bad."

"She's going to need to take this medication," Dotty said, distracting Mitch. The nurse rattled off a list of what sounded like complicated instructions. Possibly because he looked confused and uncertain, Dotty wrote everything down and reviewed it with him a second time.

"I can take her home?" he asked.

"Sure," Dotty said. "If you have any questions, feel free to call me or Angie."

"Thanks, I will."

"Can I go home now?" Chrissie asked.

"We're on our way, pumpkin."

"I want Ms. Ross to come with us. Please, Daddy, I want Ms. Ross."

Any argument he might have offered died at the pleading note in Chrissie's voice. There was very little he could have denied his daughter in that moment.

When they arrived at the house and went inside, Chrissie climbed on Bethany's lap, and soon her eyelids drifted shut.

"How'd it happen?" Mitch asked tersely, sitting across from Bethany. Even now, the thought of losing his child made him go cold with the worst fear he'd ever experienced. When he'd found Lori dead, he hadn't felt the panic that overcame him when a terrified Bethany had told him his daughter was hurt.

"I'm not sure myself how it happened," Bethany said. "As she always does on Fridays, Chrissie offered to clean the boards and erasers. My guess is that she took them outside and slipped. She must have cut her leg on the side of the Dumpster. One of the other children came running to get me."

"Thank God you were close at hand."

Bethany squeezed her eyes shut and nodded. When she opened them again, he noticed how warm and gentle they were as she looked down at Chrissie. "I don't mind telling you, it shook me, finding her like that," Bethany admitted. "You have a very special child, Mitch."

"I know." And he did. He felt a strange and unfamiliar blend of emotions as he gazed at the two of them together. One he loved beyond life itself. The other he *wanted* to love, and couldn't. He had nothing to offer her—not his heart, not marriage. And it was because he'd failed Lori, just as she'd failed herself. And failed him, failed her daughter. Day in and day out, his wife had grown more desperate, more unhappy. Following Chrissie's birth, she'd fallen into a deep depression. Nothing he said or did had helped, and he'd finally given up. Mitch blamed himself; his resignation had cost Lori her life.

"She's fast asleep," Bethany whispered, smoothing Chrissie's hair away from her temple. Her words freed him from his bitter memories and returned him to the present.

Mitch stood, gently lifting his daughter from Bethany's arms. He carried her into her bedroom while Bethany went ahead to turn down the covers, then placed his daughter in her bed.

As soundlessly as possible they left the room, keeping the door half-open.

There wasn't any excuse for Bethany to linger. She had a date with another man—but Mitch didn't want her to leave.

"I suppose you have to get ready for your dinner with John?" he said, tucking his hands in his back pockets.

"No." Her eyes held his and she slowly shook her head.

It was on the tip of his tongue to ask why, but he quickly decided he shouldn't question the unexpected gift that had been dropped in his lap.

"Chrissie and I rented a video to watch tomorrow," he said, hoping to hide his eagerness for her company. "We generally do that on weekends. This week's feature presentation is a three-year-old romantic comedy. Not my choice," he felt obliged to tell her. "Pete Livengood's movie selection isn't the most up-to-date, but I think you'd enjoy it. Would you care to stay and watch it with me?"

She gave a small, tentative smile and nodded.

Heaven knew, Mitch wanted her to stay. About as much as he'd wanted anything in his life.

"How about some popcorn?" she asked.

He grinned almost boyishly. "You got it."

It wasn't until the kernels were sizzling in the hot oil that he realized they hadn't bothered with dinner. It didn't matter. He'd fix something later if they were hungry. He had several hours before his patrol, and he didn't intend to waste them.

When the corn had finished popping, he drenched it with melted butter, then carried the two heaping bowls into the living room. Bethany followed with tall, ice-filled glasses of soda. He set the bowls on the coffee table and reached for the remote control.

Normally he would have sat in the easy chair and propped his feet on the ottoman. He chose to sit next to Bethany, instead. For this one night, he was going to indulge himself. He needed her.

The movie began, and he eased closer to her on the comfortable padded sofa. He found himself laughing out loud at the actors' farcical antics and clever banter, which was something he didn't do often. Very rarely did he see the humor in things anymore. When he ran out of popcorn, Bethany offered him some of hers. Soon his arm was around her, and she was leaning her head against his shoulder. This was about as close to heaven as he expected to get anytime within the next fifty years.

Curiously time seemed to slow, not that Mitch objected. At one comical moment in the movie, Bethany glanced at him, laughing. Her eyes were a remarkably rich shade of brown. He wondered briefly if their color intensified in moments of passion.

He swallowed hard and jerked his head away. Such thoughts were dangerous and he knew it. He reverted his attention to the television screen. Another mistake. The scene, between the hero and heroine, played by two well-known actors, was the final one of the movie, and it was a love scene.

Mitch watched as the hero's lips moved over the heroine's, first in a slow, easy kiss, then with building passion. The actors were damn good at their craft. It didn't take much to convince Mitch that the two characters they played were going to end up in the bedroom.

His breathing grew shallow as a painful longing sliced through him. The scene reminded Mitch of what he would never have with Bethany. In the same second, he realized with gut-wrenching clarity how much he wanted to kiss her.

As though neither one of them could help it, their eyes met. In Bethany's he read an aching need. And he knew that what he saw might well be a reflection of his own.

There was a long silence as the credits rolled across the screen.

It was either throw caution to the winds and kiss her— or get the hell out while he could still resist her. Almost without making a conscious decision, Mitch leapt from the sofa.

He buried his hands deep in his pockets, because he couldn't trust them not to reach for her. "Good movie, wasn't it?" he asked.

"Wonderful," she agreed, but she couldn't hide the disappointment in her voice.

"MOM, I'M SO SORRY." Lanni Caldwell stood in the doorway of the Anchorage hospital room. Her grandmother had died there only an hour before. "I came the minute I heard."

Kate looked up from her mother's bedside, her eyes filled with tears, and smiled faintly. "Thank you for getting here so quickly." Lanni's father stood behind his wife, his hand on her shoulder.

Lanni gazed at Catherine Fletcher, the woman on the bed. *Grammy*. A term of affection for a woman Lanni barely knew, but one she would always love. Her heart ached at the sight of her dead grandmother. Over the past three months, Catherine's health had taken a slow but steady turn for the worse. Yet even in her failing physical condition, Catherine had insisted she would return to Hard Luck. Dead or alive.

She would return.

Not because it was her home, but because Catherine wanted to go back to David O'Halloran, the man she'd loved for a lifetime. The man who'd left her standing at the altar more than fifty years earlier, when he'd brought home an English bride. The man she'd alternately loved and hated all these years.

"My mother's gone," Kate whispered brokenly. "She didn't even have the decency to wait for me. Like everything else in her life, she had to do this on her own. Alone. Without family."

After spending the summer in Hard Luck, Lanni better understood her mother's pain. For reasons Lanni would never fully grasp, Catherine Fletcher had given up custody of Kate when she was only a toddler. In a time when such decisions were rare, Catherine had chosen to be separated from her daughter. Chosen, instead, to stand impatiently on the sidelines waiting for David's marriage to Ellen to disintegrate. When that didn't happen, Catherine had decided to help matters along. But Ellen and David had clung steadfastly to each other, and in the end, Catherine, following David's untimely death, had let her bitterness and disillusionment take control.

All her life, Kate Caldwell had been deprived of her mother's love. She'd known that her mother had married her father on the rebound. The marriage had lasted less than two years, and Kate's birth had been unplanned, a mistake.

"Matt's on his way," Lanni told her parents. She'd spoken to her brother briefly when he phoned to give her his flight schedule. Sawyer O'Halloran was flying him into Fairbanks, and he'd catch the first available flight to Anchorage that evening. Lanni had arranged to pick him up at the airport.

After saying her own farewell to her grandmother, Lanni moved into the empty waiting room, reserved for family, to wait for her parents. Her heart felt heavy, burdened with her mother's loss more than her own.

Light footsteps alerted her to the fact that she was no longer alone. When she glanced up, she discovered Charles O'Halloran.

"Oh, Charles," she whispered, jumping to her feet. She needed his comfort now, and before another moment had passed, she was securely wrapped in his embrace.

The sobs that shook her came as a shock. Charles held her close, his strength absorbing her pain, his love quieting her grief.

"How'd you know?" Although tempted, she hadn't phoned him even though he was currently working out of Valdez.

"Sawyer."

She should have guessed his brother would tell him.

"Why didn't you call me?" he asked, tenderly smoothing the hair away from her face.

"I...didn't think I should."

Her answer appeared to surprise him. "Why not?"

"Because...I know how you still feel about Grammy. I don't blame you. She hurt you and your family."

They sat down together and Charles gripped both of Lanni's hands in his own. "I stopped hating her this summer. How could I despise the woman who was indirectly responsible for giving me you?"

Lanni swiped at the tears on her cheeks and offered a shaky smile to this man she loved to the very depths of her soul.

"And after my mother told me the circumstances that led to her marrying my dad," Charles went on, "I have a better understanding of the heartache Catherine suffered. My father made a noble sacrifice when he married Ellen. I know he grew to love her. But in his own way, I believe he always loved Catherine."

"I'd like to think they're together now," Lanni said. Charles's father and her grandmother. "This time, forever."

"I'd like to think they are too," Charles said softly, and he dropped a gentle kiss on the top of her head.

Lanni pressed her face against his shoulder and closed her eyes.

"The memorial service will be in Hard Luck?" he asked.

"Yes. And Grammy asked that her ashes be scattered on the tundra next spring."

He nodded. "Do you know when the service is?"

"No." The details had yet to be decided. Lanni lifted her head and looked up at him. "I'm glad you came."

"I'm glad I did, too. I love you, Lanni. Don't ever hold anything back from me, understand?"

She nodded.

He stood, offering her his hand. "Now let's go see about meeting your brother's plane."

MITCH HEARD via the grapevine that Bethany had a date with Bill Landgrin. His pipeline crew was working at the pump station south of Atigun Pass. The men responsible for the care and upkeep of the pipeline usually worked seven days on and seven days off. During his off-time, Bill occasionally made his way into the smaller towns that dotted the Alaskan interior.

What he came looking for was a little action. Gambling. Drinking. Every now and again, he went in search of a woman.

Mitch didn't know when or how Bill Landgrin had met Bethany. One thing was sure—Mitch didn't like the idea of his seeing Bethany. In fact, he didn't want the man anywhere near her.

Mitch understood all too well Landgrin's attraction to Bethany. It had been hard enough to idly sit by and watch her date John Henderson. The pilot was no real threat; Bill Landgrin, on the other hand, was smooth as silk and sharp as a tack. A real conniver, Mitch thought grimly.

There was no help for it. He was obligated to warn Bethany of Bill's reputation. *Someone* had to.

He bided his time, waiting until two days before she was said to be meeting Bill. As if it was a spur-of-the-moment decision, he'd stop by to see her after school. He'd make up some fiction about being concerned with Chrissie's grades—which were excellent.

He waited until he could be sure there was no chance of running into Chrissie. The last thing he needed was to have his daughter catch him seeking out Bethany's company. The kid might get the wrong idea.

Mitch had intentionally avoided Bethany since the night of Chrissie's accident. There was only so much temptation a man could take, and that evening had stretched his endurance to the breaking point.

He found Bethany sitting at her desk. Her eyes widened with surprise as he walked into the classroom. "Mitch, hello! It's good to see you."

He smiled briefly. "I hope you don't mind, my stopping in like this."

"Of course not."

"It's about Chrissie," he said hurriedly, for fear Bethany would get the wrong impression. "I've been a little, uh, concerned about her grades."

"But she's excelled in all her subjects. She's getting top marks."

He was well aware that his excuse was weak. From the moment school had started, he hadn't had to hound Chrissie to do her homework. Not even once. She would've gladly done assignments five hours a night if it meant pleasing Ms. Ross.

"I've been wondering about her grades since the accident," he said.

"They're fine." Bethany flipped through her grade book and reviewed the most recent entries. "I've kept a close eye on her, looking for any of the symptoms Dotty mentioned, but so far everything's been great. Is there a problem at home—I mean, has she been dizzy or anything like that?"

"No. No," he was quick to reassure her.

"Oh, good." She seemed relieved, and he felt even more of a fool.

Mitch stood abruptly and turned as if to leave. "By the way," he said, trying to make it sound like an afterthought, "I don't mean to pry, but did I hear correctly? Rumor has it you're having dinner with Bill Landgrin this Friday night."

"Yes." She stared at him. "How'd you know that?"

"Oh," he said with a nonchalant shrug, "word has a way of getting around. I didn't know you two had met."

"Only briefly. He was on a flight with Duke and stopped in at the café the same time I was there," she explained.

"I see," he said thoughtfully. He started to leave, then turned back with a dramatic flourish. "What about John? Do you often date men you've just met?"

"What about him?"

"Why aren't you seeing him anymore?"

Bethany hesitated. "I don't think I like the tone of your question, Mitch. I have every right to date whomever I wish."

"Yes, of course. I didn't mean to imply anything else. It's just that, well, if you must know, Bill has something of a...reputation."

She stiffened. "Thank you for your concern, but I can take care of myself."

He was making a mess of this. "I didn't mean to offend you, Bethany. It's just that I'm all this town's got in the way of law enforcement, and I thought it was my duty to warn you."

"I see." She snapped the grade book shut. "And I'm a policeman's daughter. As I told you earlier, I can take care of myself." She made a production of looking at her watch. "Now if you'll excuse me?"

"Yes, of course," he said miserably, turning to go. And this time he left.

BETHANY WASN'T SURE why she was so angry with Mitch. Possibly because he was right. She had no business having dinner with a man she barely knew. Oh, she'd be safe enough. Not much was going to happen to her in the Hard Luck Café with half the town looking on.

It went without saying that she'd agreed to this dinner date for all the wrong reasons. John Henderson had started seeing another woman recently. One of the newer recruits, a shy young woman named Sally McDonald.

After nearly six weeks here, Bethany had to conclude that Mitch didn't want to become romantically involved. The night of Chrissie's accident, she'd felt certain they'd broken through whatever barrier separating them. Even now, she remembered the way his eyes had held hers following the love scene in the movie. Bethany knew darn well what he was thinking, because she was thinking it, too. Then, when things looked the most promising, Mitch had leapt away from her as if he'd been scorched. Since then, he'd had nothing to say to her. Bethany was left feeling frustrated and confused.

When Bill Landgrin had asked her out, she'd found a dozen reasons to accept. She'd always been curious about the Alaska pipeline. It was said to stretch more than eight hundred miles across three mountain ranges and over thirteen bridges. Having dinner with a man who could answer her questions seemed innocent enough.

In addition, it sent a message to Mitch, one he'd apparently received loud and clear. He didn't like the idea of her dating Bill Landgrin, and frankly she was glad. Unfortunately Mitch had to use his daughter's injury as an excuse to talk to her about Bill. That was what irritated Bethany most.

MITCH HONESTLY TRIED to stay away from Bethany on Friday night. Chrissie was spending the night at Susan's, and the house had never seemed so empty. By seven o'clock, the walls were closing in so tightly he'd had to grab his coat and flee.

He tried to look casual and unconcerned when he walked into Ben's café. A quick look around, and his mouth filled with the bitter taste of disappointment. Bethany was nowhere in sight.

"Looking for the new teacher, are you?" Ben asked as he dried a glass with a crisp linen cloth.

"What gives you that idea?" Mitch growled. He was in no mood for conversation. "I came here for a piece of pie."

"I thought you decided to cut back on sweets."

"I changed my mind," Mitch argued. If he'd known Ben was going to be such a pain in the butt, he would've stayed at home.

Ben brought him a slice of apple pie. "In case you're interested, she left not more than twenty minutes ago."

"Who?" he asked, pretending he didn't know.

"She wasn't alone, either. Bill insisted on seeing her home."

Agitated, Mitch slapped his fork down on the plate. "Who Bethany Ross dates is her own damn business."

"Maybe," Ben said, bracing both hands against the counter, "but I don't trust the man, and you don't either, otherwise you wouldn't be here. My feeling is maybe one of us should check up on Bethany—see that everything's the way it should be."

Mitch was convinced there was more to this scenario than Ben was telling him. His blood started to heat.

"Since you're the law in this town, I think you ought to go make sure she got home all safe and sound."

Mitch wiped his mouth with the back of his hand. Ben was right. If anything happened to Bethany, Mitch would never forgive himself. In the meantime, if he did meet up with Bill, he'd impress upon the man that he was to keep away from Bethany.

"So, are you going to see her?"

No use lying about it. "Yeah."

"Then the pie's on the house," Ben said, grinning.

Mitch drove to Bethany's, grateful to see that the lights were still on. He knocked loudly on the door and would have barged in if she hadn't opened it when she did.

"Mitch?"

"May I come in?"

"Of course." She stepped aside.

He walked in and looked around. If Bill was there, he saw no evidence of it.

She'd been combing her hair, and the brush was still in her hand. She didn't ask Mitch why he'd come.

He suspected she knew.

"Did Landgrin try anything?" Mitch demanded.

Her eyes narrowed as if she didn't understand the question.

"Landgrin. Did he try anything?" he repeated gruffly.

She blinked. "No. He was a perfect gentleman."

Mitch shoved his fingers though his hair as he paced the confines of her small living room. He didn't need anyone to tell him what a fool he was making of himself.

"Will you be seeing him again?"

"That's my business."

He closed his eyes and nodded. Certainly he had no argument. "Sorry," he said. "I shouldn't have come." He stalked toward the door, eager to escape.

"Mitch?"

His hand was on the doorknob. He stopped but didn't turn around.

"I won't be seeing Bill Landgrin again."

Relief coursed through him.

"Mitch?"

She was close, so very close. He could feel her breath against the back of his neck. All he had to do was turn and she'd be there. His arms ached to hold her. His hand tightened on the doorknob as though it were a lifeline.

"I won't see Bill again," she said in a voice so soft he had to strain to hear, "because I'd much rather be seeing you."

CHAPTER FIVE

A WEEK FOLLOWING Catherine Fletcher's death, the town held a memorial service. Although she'd never met Catherine, Bethany felt obliged to attend. She slipped into the crowded church and took a place in the last row, one of the only seats left. It seemed everyone in Hard Luck wanted to say a formal goodbye to the woman who'd had such a strong impact on their community.

The moment news of Catherine's death had hit town, it was all anyone could talk about. Apparently the woman's parents had been the second family to settle in Hard Luck. Bethany knew that Catherine had grown up with David O'Halloran, although a lot of the history between the two families remained unclear to her. But it was obvious that Catherine Fletcher had played a major role in shaping the town. Folks either loved her or hated her, but either way, they respected her feisty opinions and gutsy spirit.

The mood was somber, the sense of loss keen. Hard Luck was laying to rest a piece of its heart.

A number of people attending the service were strangers to Bethany. The members of Catherine's family had flown in for the memorial. An older couple she assumed was Catherine's daughter and son-in-law. Matt Caldwell, Catherine's grandson, lived in Hard Luck. Bethany had met him one Saturday afternoon at Ben's café. She remembered that Matt had bought out the partially burned lodge from the O'Hallorans and was currently working on the repairs.

When they'd met, Matt had told her he planned to open the lodge in time for the tourist traffic next June. It was on Bethany's mind to ask *what* tourist traffic, but she hadn't.

Matt's younger sister, Lanni, sat in the front pew, as well, Charles O'Halloran close by. Bethany had heard that they were engaged, with their wedding planned for sometime in April. Even from this distance, she could see how much in love they were. It was evident from the tender looks they shared and the protective stance Charles took at his fiancée's side.

Abbey had told her about Sawyer's older brother and Lanni, and a little of the story about O'Halloran brothers' father and Catherine Fletcher. Bethany gathered that for many years there'd been no love lost between Catherine and the O'Hallorans. Then again, she thought, perhaps that *was* the problem between the two families. *Love lost.* Maybe, just maybe, it had been found again through Charles and Lanni.

Silently Bethany applauded them for having the courage to seek out their happiness, despite the past.

Reverend Wilson, the circuit minister, had flown in for the service. He stepped forward, clutching his Bible, and began the service with a short prayer. Bethany solemnly bowed her head. No sooner had the prayer ended than Mitch Harris slipped into the pew beside her.

He didn't acknowledge her in any way. She could have been a stranger for all the attention he gave her. His attitude stung. It hurt to realize that if there'd been anyplace else to sit, he would have taken it.

As the service progressed, Bethany noticed how restless Mitch became. He shifted his position a number of times, almost as though he was in some discomfort. When she dared to look his way, she discovered that his eyes were closed and his hands tightly clenched into fists.

Then it hit her.

She knew little of his life, but she did know that he was a widower.

Reverend Wilson opened his Bible and read from the Twenty-third Psalm. "'Yea, though I walk through the valley of the shadow of death, I will fear no evil: for thou art with me; thy rod and thy staff they comfort me.'"

Mitch had traversed that dark, lonely valley himself, and Bethany speculated that he hadn't found the comfort the pastor spoke of. And she realized, as Reverend Wilson continued, that it wasn't Catherine Fletcher Mitch mourned. It was his dead wife. The woman he'd loved. And married. The woman who'd carried his child. The woman he couldn't forget.

How foolish she'd been! Mitch didn't want to become involved with her. How could he when he remained emotionally tied to his dead wife? No wonder he'd been fighting her so hard. He was trapped somewhere in the past, shackled to a memory, a dead love.

Bethany closed her eyes, amazed that it had taken her so long to see what should have been obvious. True, he was attracted to her. That much neither could deny. But he wasn't free to love her. Maybe he didn't *want* to be free. He probably hated himself for even thinking about someone else. His behavior at this memorial service explained everything.

Mitch leaned forward, supporting his elbows on his knees, and hid his face in his hands. He was in such unmistakable pain that Bethany couldn't sit idly by and do nothing. Not knowing whether her gesture would be welcome, she drew a deep breath and gently laid her hand on his forearm.

He jerked himself upright and swiveled in his seat to look at her. Surprise blossomed in his eyes. Apparently he'd forgotten he was sitting next to her. She gave him a slight smile, wanting him to know only that she was his friend. Nothing more.

Mitch blinked, and his face filled with a vulnerability that tore at her heart. She wanted to help, but she didn't know how.

As if reading her thoughts, Mitch reached out and grasped her hand. The touch had nothing to do with physical desire. He'd come to her in his pain.

Then, as if he couldn't bear it any longer, he rose abruptly and hurried out of the church. Bethany twisted around and watched him leave, the doors slamming behind him.

MITCH STALKED into his office, his chest heaving as if the short walk had demanded intense physical effort. His heart hammered wildly and his breathing was labored.

He'd decided at the last minute to attend the memorial service. He hadn't known Catherine Fletcher well, but appreciated the contribution she and her family had made to the community.

Mitch had talked with her only a few times in the past five years. Nevertheless he'd seen his attendance at the service as a social obligation, a way of paying his respects.

But the minute he'd walked into the church, he'd been bombarded with memories of Lori. They'd come at him from all sides, closing in on him until he thought he'd suffocate.

He remembered the day he'd first met her and how attracted he'd been to the delightful sound of her laughter. They'd been college sophomores, still young and inexperienced. Then they'd gotten married; they'd had the large, traditional wedding she'd wanted and he'd never seen a more beautiful bride. They were deeply in love, blissfully happy. At least he'd been. In the beginning.

When they learned she was pregnant, a new joy, unlike anything he'd experienced before, had taken hold of him. But after Chrissie was born, their lives had quickly slid downhill. Mitch covered his head. He didn't want to remember any more.

He continued to pace in the silence of his office. Attending the memorial service had been a mistake. He'd suffered the backlash caused by years of refusing to deal with the pain. Years of denial. Now he felt as though he were collapsing inward.

He'd never felt so desperate, so out of control.

"Mitch."

He whirled around. Bethany stood just inside the office, her eyes full of compassion.

"Are you all right?"

He nodded, soundlessly telling her nothing was wrong. Even as he did, he realized he couldn't sustain the lie. "No," he said in a choked whisper.

Slowly she advanced into the room. "What is it?"

He closed his eyes and shook his head. His throat clogged. He stood defenseless as his control crumpled.

Gently Bethany's hand fell on his arm. He might have been able to resist her comfort if she hadn't touched him. His body reacted immediately to the physical contact, and he lurched as if her hand had stung him. Only it wasn't pain he experienced, but an incredible sense of release.

"Let me hold you...please," he said. "I need...I need you." He didn't wait for her permission before he brought her into his arms and buried his face in her shoulder. She was soft and warm. Alive. He drew in several great lungfuls of air, hoping that would help stabilize his erratic heart.

"Everything's all right," she whispered, her lips close to his ear. "Don't worry."

Her arms were his shelter, his protection. The first time he'd met Bethany, he'd promised himself he wouldn't become involved with her. Until now he'd steadfastly stuck to that vow.

But he hadn't counted on needing her—or anyone—this badly. She was his sanity.

He knew he was going to kiss her in the same moment he acknowledged how desperate he'd been for her. With a hoarse groan that came from deep in his throat he surrendered to a need so strong he couldn't possibly have refused it.

Their lips met, and it was like a burst of spontaneous combustion. He'd waited so long. He needed her so badly. One hand gathering the blond thickness of her unbound hair, he kissed her repeatedly, working his mouth over hers, unable to get enough.

He feared his astonishing need had shocked her, and he sighed with heartfelt relief when she opened her mouth to him, welcoming the invasion of his tongue.

He moaned, wanting to tell her how sorry he was. But he was unwilling to break the contact, to leave her for even those short seconds.

Bethany coiled her arms tightly about his neck. Again and again he ran his hands down the length of her spine, savoring the feel of this woman in his arms. Their mouths worked urgently, frantically, against each other. He felt insatiable, and she responded with an intensity that equaled his own.

Mitch broke off the kiss when it became more than he could physically handle. He felt that the passion between them might never have burned itself out. At the rate things had progressed, the kiss would quickly have taken them toward something more intimate. Something neither one of them was ready to deal with yet.

Bethany gasped in an effort to catch her breath, and she pressed her hand over her heart as though to still its frenzied beat. Her lips were swollen. Mitch raised his index finger and gently stroked the slick smoothness of her mouth.

Slowly he raised his head and studied her.

She blinked, as if she was confused. Or dazed.

He was instantly filled with regret. "That should never have happened," he whispered.

She said nothing.

"I promise you it won't happen again," he continued.

Her eyes flickered with...anger? She opened her mouth, then abruptly closed it again. Before another second had passed, she'd turned and rushed out of his office.

MATT HAD FOUND the day long and emotionally exhausting. He'd attended the services for his grandmother and the wake that followed.

His mother mourned deeply, and in his own way Matt did, too. His grief surprised him. Matt had barely known Catherine—Grammy, as Lanni called her. There'd only been a few visits over the years.

She'd always sent a card with a check for his birthday. Money again at Christmas. A Bible when he graduated from high school, and a trust fund she'd established for him. This was the money he'd used to buy the lodge from the O'Halloran brothers.

His grandmother had never known how he'd used the money in the trust fund. By the time he was able to collect it this past summer, her health had disintegrated so much she no longer recognized him. Somehow Matt felt she would have condoned his choice. He liked to think she would have, anyway.

The memorial service and wake had gone well. Virtually all the townspeople had offered condolences, and many had inquired about his progress with the lodge.

The people of Hard Luck had been open and friendly since his arrival, but Matt tended to keep to himself. He was too busy getting the lodge ready to socialize much. He didn't dare stop and think about everything that needed to be done before he officially posted an Open sign on the front door. The multitude of tasks sometimes overwhelmed him.

Readying the lodge was a considerable chore, but his success depended on a whole lot more than making sure the rooms were habitable.

He'd have to convince people to make the trek this far north, and he'd have to provide them with activities. Wilderness treks, fishing, dogsledding. If his first order of business was getting the lodge prepared for paying customers, his second was attracting said customers.

He'd do it. Come hell or high water or both. By God, he'd do it. He had something to prove to—

His mind came to an abrupt halt.

Karen.

He worked fifteen-hour days for one reason, and that reason was Karen. Just saying her name produced an aching sensation in his heart, an ache that had started the day she'd filed for divorce.

What the hell kind of wife filed for divorce without discussing the subject with her husband first? Okay, so maybe she'd mentioned once or twice that she was unhappy.

Well, dammit, he was unhappy, too!

He'd be the first to admit she had a valid complaint— but only to a point. True, he'd changed careers four times in about that many years. He was a man with an eye to the future, and opportunities abounded. But Karen had accused him of being self-indulgent and irresponsible, unable to settle down. That wasn't true, though. He'd always headed on to something new when the challenge was gone, when a job no longer held his interest.

In some ways he supposed he could understand her discontent, but he'd never thought she'd actually leave him. To be fair, she'd threatened it, but he hadn't believed her.

If she truly loved him, she would have stuck it out.

Matt shook his head. There was no point in reviewing the same issues again. He'd gone over what had led to the divorce a thousand times without solving anything. It wouldn't now, either.

The final blow had been when she left Alaska. Oh, he'd fully expected her to do well in her career. She was an executive secretary for some highfalutin engineering company. Great job. Great pay. When they'd offered her a raise and a promotion, she'd leapt at the chance. Without a word, she'd packed her bags and headed for California.

For the love of God, California? Even now he had trouble believing it.

He reached for a magazine and idly flipped through the pages, then slapped it closed. Thinking about Karen was unproductive.

California! He hoped to hell she was happy.

No, he didn't. He wanted her to be miserable, as miserable as he was. Damn, but he missed her. Damn, but he loved her.

A year. You'd think he'd be over her by now. He should be seeing new women, going out, making friends. He might have, too, if he wasn't so busy working on the lodge. But if he had some free time and if there were single women available—like that new teacher, maybe—he'd start dating again.

No, he wouldn't.

Matt wasn't going to lie to himself. Not after today when he'd stood with his family and mourned the loss of his grandmother. His parents had been married nearly thirty years now, high school sweethearts. Lanni and Charles had stood on his other side. Together.

Losing Grammy had been difficult for Lanni. Having spent part of the summer in Hard Luck cleaning out their grandmother's home, Lanni felt much closer to Catherine. She grieved, and Charles was there to lend comfort.

The way his father comforted his mother.

But Matt stood alone.

It pained him to admit how much he'd yearned to have Karen beside him. His agony intensified when he was forced to recognize how deeply he still loved her.

He wondered if it would always be this way. Would he ever learn to let her go? Not that he had any real choice. The truth was, any day now he expected to hear she'd remarried.

There wasn't a damn thing to stop her. The men in California would have to be blind not to notice her. It wouldn't take long for her to link up with some executive who'd give her the stability she craved. There wasn't a man alive who could resist her, he thought morosely. He should know.

His ex-wife was beautiful, talented, generous and spirited. Was she spirited!

A smile cracked his lips. Not many people would believe that the cool, calm Karen Caldwell loved to throw things—mainly at Matt. She'd hurled the most ridiculous objects, too.

His shirt. A newspaper. Potato chips. Decorator pillows.

When her anger reached this point, there was only one sure method to cool her ire. One method that had never failed him.

He'd make love to her. The lovemaking was wild and wicked, and soon they'd both be so caught up in the sheer magic of it she'd forget whatever it was that had angered her.

Matt remembered the last time Karen had expressed her fury like a major-league pitcher. His smile widened as he leaned back in his chair and clasped his hands behind his head.

He'd quit his job. All right, he should have discussed it with her first. He hadn't planned to go into work that day and hand in his notice. It had just...happened.

Karen had been furious with him. He tried to explain that he'd found something better. Accounting wasn't for him—he should have realized it long before now. He'd been thinking about something else, something better suited to his talents.

She wouldn't give him a chance to explain. Ranting and raving, she'd started flinging whatever she could lay hands on. Matt had ducked when she'd sent her shoes flying in his direction. The saltshaker had scored a direct hit, clobbering him in the chest.

That had given her pause, he recalled, but not for long. Braving her anger, he'd advanced toward her. She'd refused to let him near her. When she ran out of easy-to-reach ammunition, she'd walked across the top of the sofa and leapt onto the chair, all the while shouting at the top of her lungs and threatening him with the pepper mill.

It hadn't taken much to capture her and he'd let her yell and struggle in his arms for a few minutes. Then he did the only thing he could to silence Karen—kiss her.

Before long, the pepper mill had tumbled from her hands and onto the carpet, and they were helping each other undress, their hands as urgent as their need.

Afterward, he remembered, Karen had been quiet and still. While he lay on his back, appreciating the most incredible sex of his life, his wife had been plotting their divorce. Less than a week later, she moved out and he was served with the papers.

The smile faded as the sadness crept back into his heart.

He modified his wish. He didn't want Karen to be miserable. If someone had to be blamed, then fine, he'd accept full responsibility for their failure. He deserved it.

He missed her so much! Never more than now. Whatever happened in the future with this lodge and the success of his business venture seemed of little consequence. Matt would go to his grave loving Karen.

Like his grandmother before him, he would only love once.

"YOU'RE LOOKING PENSIVE," Sawyer said as he sat on the edge of the bed and peeled off his socks.

With her back propped against the headboard, Abbey glanced over the top of her mystery novel. "Of course I look pensive," she muttered, smiling at her husband. "I'm reading."

"You're pretending to read," he corrected. "You've got that look again."

"What look?" she asked him with an expression of pure innocence.

"The one that says you're plotting."

Abbey made a face at him. How was it Sawyer knew her so well? They hadn't been married all that long. "And what exactly am I plotting?" She'd see if he could figure *that* one out.

"I don't know, but I'm sure you'll tell me sooner or later."

"For your information, Mr. Know-It-All, I was just thinking about Thanksgiving."

Sawyer cocked his head to one side, as if to say he wasn't sure he should believe her. "That's weeks away. Tell me what could possibly be so important about Thanksgiving that it would occupy your mind now?"

"Well, for one thing, I was thinking we should ask Mitch and Chrissie to join us." She glanced at her husband in order to gauge his reaction.

Sawyer didn't hesitate. "Good idea."

"And Bethany Ross."

A full smile erupted on Sawyer's handsome face as he pointed his finger at her. "What did I say? You're plotting."

"What?" Once more she feigned innocence.

"You want to invite Mitch *and* Bethany to Thanksgiving dinner?"

"Right," she concurred, opening her eyes wide in exaggerated wonder that he could find anything the *least* bit underhand in such a courtesy. "And what, pray tell, is so devious about that?"

His finger wagged again as he climbed into bed. "A little matchmaking, maybe? You've got something up your sleeve, Abbey O'Halloran."

"I most certainly do not," she said with a touch of righteous indignation.

"I notice you didn't suggest inviting John Henderson."

"No," she admitted.

"Isn't he the one Bethany's been having dinner with the last few weeks?"

"They're friends, that's all."

"I see." Sawyer leaned over and deftly reached for one end of the satin ribbon tying the collar of her pajama top. He slowly tugged until it fell open.

"Besides, I heard from Mariah that John's interested in someone else now."

Sawyer idly unfastened the first button of her top. "Is that right?"

Her husband's touch was warm, creating feathery sensations that scampered across her skin.

Sawyer's eyes dropped to her mouth, and his voice lowered to a soft purr. "Mitch has lived here for a number of years now."

"True." Her second button gave way as easily as the first.

"If he was interested in remarrying, he'd have done something about it before now, wouldn't you think?"

Abbey closed her book and set it blindly on the table next to the bed. "Not necessarily."

"Do you think Mitch is interested in Bethany?" Sawyer slipped his hand inside the opening he'd created.

Abbey closed her eyes at the feel of her husband's fingers. "Yes." The word sounded shockingly intimate.

"As it happens," Sawyer said in a husky whisper, "I agree with you."

"You do?" Her voice dwindled to a whisper. With her eyes still closed, she swayed toward him.

Sawyer's kiss was long and deep. The conversation about Mitch Harris and Bethany Ross stopped there. Instead, Sawyer and Abbey continued their dialogue with husky sighs and soft murmurs.

BETHANY WALKED into the Hard Luck Café shortly after ten on Saturday and sat at the counter. The place was empty of customers. Ben wasn't in sight, either, which was fine; she wasn't in any hurry. Tired of her own company, she'd decided to take a walk and sort through what had happened between her and Mitch. Ha! she thought sourly. As if such a thing was possible.

There wasn't anyone she could ask about Mitch's past. And apparently *he* wasn't going to volunteer the information. He hadn't said word one about his life before Hard Luck, and no one else seemed to know much, either.

As for what had happened at the memorial service, Bethany had given up any attempt to make sense of it. For whatever reason, Mitch had turned to her. He'd kissed her with such intensity, such hunger, that her heart had burst open with an incredible sense of joy.

Then he'd apologized. And she'd realized he had simply needed someone. Anyone. Any woman would have sufficed. She just happened to be handy. The minute he saw what he'd done, he regretted ever having touched her.

"Bethany, hello! How are you this fine day?" As always, Ben greeted her with a wide smile as he bustled up to the counter. "We missed you at the wake after Catherine's memorial service. The women in town put on a mighty fine spread."

There was probably some psychological significance in the fact that she'd seek out Ben now, Bethany decided. If she wasn't so sick of analyzing the situation between her and Mitch, she might have delved into *that* question. As it was, she felt too miserable to care.

"I'm fine."

"Is that so?" Without her asking, Ben filled a mug with coffee. "Then why are those little lines I see between your eyes?"

"What lines?"

He pointed to his own forehead. "When I'm stewing about something, these lines magically appear on my brow. Three of them. Seems to me you're cursed with the same thing. Can't fool a living soul, no matter how hard I try." He smiled, encouraging her to talk.

Bethany resisted the urge to tell him she'd come by those lines honestly. Inhaling a deep breath, she eyed him, wondering how much she dared confide in him about her feelings for Mitch. Darn little, she suspected. That she'd even wonder was a sign of how desperate she'd become.

"What can you tell me about Mitch?" she asked.

"Mitch? Mitch Harris?" All at once, Ben found it necessary to wipe down the counter. He ran a rag over the top of the already spotless surface. "Well, for one thing, he's a damn good man. Decent, caring. Loves his daughter."

"He's lived in Hard Luck for how long?" She already knew the answer, but she wanted to ease Ben into the conversation.

"Must be five years now. Maybe a little longer."

She nodded. "I heard he worked for the police department in Chicago before that."

"That's what I heard, too."

"Do you know how his wife died?" Since Ben wasn't going to volunteer any real information, she'd have to pry it out of him.

"Can't say I do." His mouth twisted to one side, as if he was judging what he should and shouldn't tell her. "I don't think Mitch has ever talked about her to anyone. Hasn't mentioned her to me."

Bethany heard the door open behind her. Their conversation was over, not that she'd gleaned any new information.

"If you're curious about his wife," Ben whispered, "I suggest you ask him yourself. He just walked in."

For the briefest of seconds, she felt like a five-year-old with her hand caught in the cookie jar.

To her surprise, Mitch opted to sit on the stool next to hers. He studied her for what seemed an eternity. "Hello, Bethany," he finally said in a low voice.

"Mitch." She refused to meet his eyes.

"I'm glad I ran into you."

Well, that was certainly a change.

Ben strolled over and Mitch asked for coffee.

"I'd like to talk to you, Bethany." He gestured toward one of the booths, the steaming mug in his hand.

She followed him to the farthest booth, and they sat across from each other. For long moments, he didn't say anything, and when he lifted his head to look at her, his eyes were bleak.

"Bethany, I can't tell you how sorry I am. I don't know what else to say. I've lain awake nights worrying what you must think of me."

Confused and hurt, Bethany said nothing.

He gestured helplessly. "I'm sorry. What more can I say? Talk to me, would you? Say something. Anything."

"What are you sorry for?" she asked, her voice almost a whisper. "Kissing me?"

"Yes."

Even now he didn't seem to realize she'd been a willing participant. "You needed me. Was that why?"

"Yes," he said, as if this was his greatest sin.

She hesitated, searching for the words. "Any other woman would have done just as well. Isn't that what you're really saying? It wasn't *me* you were kissing. It wasn't *me* you needed. I just happened to . . . be available."

CHAPTER SIX

"YOU'RE GOING to do it, aren't you?" Duke Porter asked John for the second time. An incredulous look contorted the pilot's features. "You're *actually* going to do it?"

"Yes," John said, irritated. He jerked the grease rag from his back pocket and brusquely wiped his hands.

Duke followed him to the far end of the hangar while John put away the tools he'd used. "You're sure this is what you want?"

John didn't hesitate. "I'm absolutely, positively sure."

"But you barely know the woman."

"I know everything I need to know," he muttered. Duke was good at raising his hackles, but nothing was going to ruin this day. The engagement ring burned a hole in his pocket. The searing eagerness to propose was nothing compared to the way he felt about Sally.

This time it was *his* turn. Earlier, he'd fallen all over himself in an attempt to court Abbey Sutherland. What he hadn't known was that Sawyer O'Halloran had stolen her heart without giving any of the others a chance.

Then there was Lanni Caldwell. John had never seriously considered her wife material, believing she'd only be in town for the summer. Duke might have been more interested in striking up a relationship with her, but once again they'd been beaten out by one of the O'Halloran brothers.

John liked Mariah Douglas well enough, but it was plain as the nose on your face that she only had eyes for Christian. Besides, the last thing he wanted to do was tangle with *her*. Daddy Douglas just might sic that attorney on him.

He'd had a shot with Bethany, the schoolteacher. In the beginning he was quite drawn to her. He knew she didn't share his enthusiasm, but he'd figured that, given time, their friendship might grow into something more.

Then Sally McDonald had arrived.

Sally, with her pretty blue eyes and her gentle smile. He'd taken one look at her and his heart had stopped beating. In that moment, he'd recognized beyond a hint of a doubt that she was the one for him. After John had met Sally, he didn't resent Sawyer for stealing Abbey away from him and the others. It seemed like a little thing that Lanni was marrying Charles, or that Bethany Ross wasn't as keen on him as he'd been on her. Sally was the one for him.

"If you want my opinion . . ."

John glared at Duke. "I didn't ask for it, did I?"

"No," Duke argued, "but I'm going to give it to you anyway."

John sighed loudly. "All right. If you find it so important, tell me what you think."

"I can understand why you'd want to marry Sally—" Duke began.

"But you're thinking about her for yourself!" This explained why Duke was poking into something that was none of his concern.

"No way," Duke said, raising both hands. "I'm off women. Too many of 'em are like that lawyer, looking for any excuse to chew on a man's butt."

"Tracy Santiago wasn't like that." John grinned broadly at the memory of the way those two had clashed. To be fair, he wasn't interested in her for himself, but he kinda liked the way she'd cut Duke down to size. "She was doing her job, that's all."

"Listen, if you don't mind, I'd rather not discuss that she-devil. She's gone, at least for now, and all I can say is good riddance. The woman was nothing but a damned nuisance."

John swallowed back a laugh. He'd never seen Duke get this riled up over a woman. It seemed to his inexperienced eye that his friend protested too much. He figured that, this time, Duke had met his match. Too bad Tracy lived in Washington State and Duke in Alaska.

"About Sally..." The other pilot broached the topic once more.

John could see there was no escaping his friend's unwanted counsel. "All right," he said, giving in. Duke was going to state his opinion whether John wanted to hear it or not. He might as well listen—or pretend to.

"Don't get me wrong here," Duke said, and stuffed his hands in his pockets as though he found this matter difficult. "I like Sally. Who wouldn't? She's a real sweetheart."

"Exactly."

"The thing that concerns me is...she's young."

"Not that much younger than Bethany. Or Lanni."

"True, only Sally's led a more sheltered life than either of them."

John found he couldn't disagree. Sally had been raised in a British Columbia town with a population of less than a thousand. From what he understood, her family was a closeknit one. She'd attended a small, private high school and a church-affiliated college. When finances became too tight for her to continue her education, she'd gotten a job working in an accounting office in Vancouver. That was where she'd read Christian's newspaper ad and applied for the job with Hard Luck Power and Light.

"You know why she came to Hard Luck, don't you?"

"Yeah." John knew, and frankly he was surprised Duke did, too. After moving to Vancouver, Sally had become involved with a fast-talking man who'd ultimately broken her heart. He'd been married; she'd found out because his wife had shown up at her door.

According to what she'd told him, Sally had walked away from the relationship feeling both heartsick and foolish. When she read about Midnight Sons offering land, housing and jobs, she'd jumped at the opportunity to start over. This time she'd do it in a small-town environment, the sort she was familiar and comfortable with.

"Are you sure she's over this other guy?" Duke asked.

"I'm sure." Although he made it sound like there could be no question, John wasn't entirely convinced. He was grateful Duke didn't challenge his response.

"What about her family?" the other pilot asked, instead.

"What about them?" John said defensively. He didn't much like where Duke's questions were leading.

"From what you've said, they're the old-fashioned sort. If you're serious about marrying their daughter, the thing to do is talk to her father first. Meet him face-to-face and tell him how you love Sally and—"

"How the hell am I supposed to do that?" John wanted to know. "Sal's dad lives in some dinky town on the coast. It isn't like I can leave here. Especially now."

Winter had set in with full force. Temperatures had dipped into the minus range every day for a solid week.

When it fell to minus thirty, Midnight Sons was forced to cancel all flights. The stress to the aircraft was too great a risk.

Snow accumulations measured forty inches or more in the past month alone. Thanksgiving was less than a week away, and there didn't seem to be any break in the weather ahead. In a word, they were snowed in. No matter how much he wanted to meet Sally's family, for the time being it was impossible.

"First," Duke said, and held up his hand. He pressed down one finger. "You got a woman who's only recently turned twenty-one, so she's young. Younger than any of the others who've come to Hard Luck. Secondly—" he bent down another finger "—she moved here on the rebound, hoping to cure a broken heart."

"Third," John said, fighting back his frustration, "she comes from a family who wouldn't appreciate their daughter marrying a man they haven't personally met and approved."

"If you start out on the wrong foot with her parents, it could take you years to make up for it," Duke said. "If you truly love her—"

"I do," John insisted heatedly, then added in a lower voice, "I've never felt this strongly about anyone."

His friend nodded in understanding. "Then do this right. I can't think of a single reason to rush into marriage, can you?"

John could list any number of reasons to marry Sally that very day, but said nothing.

"If she's the one for you, then everything will work out the way it's supposed to, and you've got nothing to worry about."

John shrugged. He didn't like it, but Duke had a valid point. The engagement ring could continue to burn a hole in his pocket until he'd had a chance to square matters with Sally's father. Until he could be sure she loved him for himself—and not as an instant cure for a broken heart.

"DADDY, I DON'T FEEL GOOD." Chrissie came slowly into the kitchen, clutching her Pooh bear to her chest. The stuffed animal was a favorite from her preschool days. Now she sought it out only on rare occasions.

Concerned, Mitch stuck the casserole in the oven, then pressed the back of his hand against his daughter's brow. She did feel warm. Her face was flushed and her eyes were unusually solemn.

"What's wrong, pumpkin?"

She shrugged. "I just don't feel good."

"Does your tummy hurt?" There'd been lots of flu going around.

Chrissie nodded.

"Do you have a sore throat?"

She bobbed her head and swallowed. "It hurts there, too."

"You'd better let me take your temperature."

Her eyes flared wide. "No! I don't want that thing in my mouth."

"Chrissie, it isn't going to hurt."

"I don't care. I don't want you to take my temperature. I'll... I'll just go to bed."

Mitch had forgotten how unreasonable his daughter could be when she was ill. "Don't you feel like eating dinner?"

"No," she answered weakly. "I just want to go to bed. Don't worry about me. I won't die."

Mitch sighed. He didn't know if she was being dramatic or was expressing some kind of anxiety about death. She'd known about Catherine's funeral, and maybe that had made her think about Lori....

"Will you tuck me in?"

"Of course." He followed her down the narrow hallway to her bedroom. While he pulled back her covers, Chrissie knelt on the floor and said her prayers. It seemed to take her twice as long as usual, but Mitch pretended not to notice.

Once she was securely tucked beneath the blankets, Mitch sat on the edge of her bed and brushed the hair from her brow. Her face seemed a little warm.

"Stay with me, okay?" she asked in a voice that suggested she was fading quickly.

Mitch reached for the Jack London story he'd been reading to her. Chrissie placed her hand on his forearm to stop him. "I want you to read the story about the Princess Bride. That's my favorite."

Mitch swore he'd read the book a thousand times. Chrissie could recite parts of it from memory, and Mitch knew he could repeat whole sections of it without bothering to turn the pages. Although his daughter was quite capable of reading on her own, there were certain stories she insisted he read to her.

He picked up the book and flipped it open. He made it through the first page by merely glancing at it a few times.

"Daddy."

"Yes, pumpkin?"

"Are we going to Susan's for Thanksgiving?"

Mitch closed the book. "Sawyer asked this afternoon if we'd join them for dinner." Naturally Susan would have said something to Chrissie. Sawyer had also let it drop that Bethany would be there, then waited for his reaction. So Mitch had smiled politely and said he looked forward to seeing her again. Actually it was true.

"Did you tell Sawyer we'd come?"

Mitch nodded.

Chrissie's eyes lit up, as if this confirmation had given her a reason to live. "I hope I'm not still sick." She made a show of swallowing.

"You won't be."

Mitch didn't know what was wrong with his daughter, but he had a sneaking suspicion it wasn't nearly as serious as she'd like him to believe. He sat with her a few minutes more, then moved into the kitchen to check on dinner.

"Dad-dy!"

It was a deathbed call if ever he'd heard one. He made his way down the hallway and stuck his head inside her bedroom door. "Now what?"

"I want Ms. Ross."

Mitch's heart rate accelerated. "Why?"

Chrissie nodded. "I just want to talk to her, all right?"

Mitch hesitated. Of all the things he expected Chrissie to ask of him, Bethany wasn't it. A game of checkers. A glass of juice. Anything but her teacher.

"Please, oh, please, Daddy. Ms. Ross will make me feel *so* much better."

If Mitch was looking for an excuse to call Bethany, then his daughter had just offered it to him on a golden serving dish. They hadn't seen much of each other in the past few weeks, but Bethany seemed to be the one avoiding him. Embarrassed by what had happened in his office during Catherine Fletcher's service, Mitch had decided to let her be. He'd done enough damage.

But it didn't change the way he felt about her. They couldn't be in the same vicinity without his heart erupting. It had been years since he'd felt this vulnerable with a woman, and frankly it made him nervous.

Since their meeting at Ben's place, they'd greeted each other cordially—nothing personal. Just noncommittal chitchat, of the kind he might have exchanged with a near-stranger.

None of that, however, was enough for Mitch to forget the feel of Bethany in his arms, Bethany's lips on his, warm and welcoming. And so blessedly giving that he wanted to kick himself every time he thought about the way he'd treated her.

"Daddy." Chrissie gave him a long look. "Will you call Ms. Ross?"

He nodded helplessly. Walking into the kitchen, he reached for the phone. Chrissie couldn't possibly realize what she'd asked of him. Even while that thought formed in his mind, he realized he was grateful for the excuse to call Bethany.

He punched out the phone number and waited. Bethany answered on the second ring.

"Hello."

Now that he heard her voice, he felt a moment's panic. What could he possibly say? He didn't want to exaggerate and make it sound as if Chrissie was seriously ill, nor did he wish to make light of the request for fear that Bethany would see through it.

"It's Mitch."

No response.

"I'm sorry to trouble you."

"It's no trouble." She sounded friendly, but not overly so.

"Chrissie seems to have come down with the flu." Then, on a stroke of genius, he invented the reason for his call. "Did she mention not feeling well at school to-day?"

"No, she didn't say a word." Concern was more evident in her voice than irritation.

"It's probably nothing more than a twenty-four hour virus," he said.

"Is there anything I can do?" she asked.

He'd been born under a lucky star, Mitch decided. Without his having to say a word, she'd volunteered.

"As a matter of fact, Chrissie's feeling pretty bad at the moment and she's asking for you. I don't want you to go out of your way—"

"I'll be there in ten minutes."

"No." He wouldn't hear of her walking that far in weather this cold. "I'll come for you in the snowmobile."

She hesitated. "Fine. I'll watch for you."

Mitch went back into Chrissie's bedroom. "I talked to Ms. Ross."

"And?" Chrissie nearly fell out of the bed she was so eager to hear the outcome of the conversation.

"She'll come, but I didn't want her walking over here in the cold. I'm going to pick her up in the snowmobile. You'll be all right alone for five minutes, won't you?"

Chrissie's eyes filled with outrage. "I'm not a little kid anymore!"

"I'm glad to know that." If he'd actually been upset about asking Bethany to visit, he might have pointed out that someone who wasn't a little kid anymore wouldn't ask for her teacher.

Mitch called out to Chrissie that he was leaving. He pulled on his insulated, waterproof jacket and wound the thick scarf around his neck, covering his mouth, before he stepped outside. The snowmobile was the most frequently used means of transportation in the winter months, and he kept his well maintained. The minute he pulled up outside Bethany's small house, her door opened and she appeared.

She climbed onto the back of the snowmobile and positioned herself a discreet distance behind him. Nevertheless, having her this close produced a fiery warmth he couldn't escape—didn't *want* to escape.

She didn't say anything until they'd reached his house. He parked the snowmobile inside the garage and plugged in the heater to protect the engine.

Once in the house they removed their winter gear. Bethany was wearing leggings and an oversize San Francisco Police Department sweatshirt; her feet were covered in heavy red woollen socks. He stared at her, taking in every detail.

Mitch found he couldn't speak. It was the first time they'd been alone together since the scene in his office. This sudden intimacy caught him off guard, and he wasn't sure how to react.

Part of him yearned to reach for her and kiss her again. Only this time he'd be tender, drawing out the kiss with a gentle touch that would—

"Where's Chrissie?" Bethany asked, mercifully breaking into his thoughts.

"Chrissie... She's in her bedroom."

The oven timer went off, and grateful for the excuse to leave her and clear his head, Mitch walked into kitchen. He opened the oven and pulled out the ground-turkey casserole to cool on top of the stove.

He entered his daughter's room and discovered Bethany sitting on the bed, with Chrissie cuddled close. The child's head rested against Bethany's shoulder as she read from the story he'd begun himself. When Chrissie glanced up to find Mitch watching, her eyes shone with happiness.

"Hi, Dad," she said, craning her neck to look up at Bethany. "Dad usually reads me this story, but you do it better because you love it, too. I don't think Dad likes romance stories."

"Dinner's ready," Mitch announced. "Are you sure you won't try to eat something, pumpkin?"

Chrissie's frown said that was a terribly difficult decision for her to make. "Maybe I could eat just a little, but only if Ms. Ross will stay and have dinner with us."

Before Bethany could offer a perfunctory excuse, Mitch said, "There's plenty, and we'd both enjoy having you." He wanted to be certain she understood that he wouldn't object to her company; if anything he'd be glad of it.

He saw her gaze travel from Chrissie and then back to him. He leaned against the doorway, his hands deep in his pockets, trying to give the impression that it made no difference to him if she joined them for dinner or not. But it did. He wanted her to stay.

"I... It's thoughtful of you to ask. I, uh, haven't eaten yet."

"Oh, goodie." Chrissie jumped up and clapped her hands, bouncing with glee. Then, as if she'd just remembered how ill she was supposed to be, she sagged her shoulders and all but crumpled onto the bed.

In an effort to hide his smile, Mitch returned to the kitchen and quickly set the table. By the time Chrissie and Bethany joined him, he'd brought the casserole to the table, as well as a loaf of bread, butter and some straight-from-the-can bean salad.

Dinner was... an odd affair. Exciting. Fun. And a little sad. It was as if he and Bethany were attempting to find new ground with each other. Only, they both seemed to fear that this ground would be strewn with land mines. He'd take one step forward, then freeze, afraid he'd said something that might offend her.

He noticed that Bethany didn't find this new situation any easier than he did. She'd start to laugh, then her eyes, her beautiful brown eyes, would meet his and the laugh would falter.

Following their meal, Chrissie wanted her to finish the story. Since Mitch was well aware of how the story ended, he lingered in the kitchen over a cup of coffee.

He had just started the dishes when Bethany reappeared.

"Chrissie's decided she needs her beauty sleep," she told him, standing at the far side of the room.

Mitch didn't blame her for maintaining the distance between them. Every time she'd attempted to get close, he'd shoved her away. Every time she'd opened her heart to him, he'd shunned her. Yet when he'd desperately needed her, she'd been there. And although she'd accused him of settling for any woman who happened to fall into his arms, *she* was the only one who could fill the need in him.

"I imagine you want to get back home," he said, experiencing a curious sadness. He dumped what remained of his coffee into the sink. Something about the way her eyes flickered told him she might have enjoyed a cup had he offered one.

"Stay," he said suddenly. "Just for a few minutes."

The invitation seemed to hang in the air. It took her a long time to decide; when he was about to despair, she offered him a small smile, then nodded.

"Coffee?"

"Please."

His heart reacted with a wild burst of staccato beats. He quickly poured her a mug, grabbing a fresh one for himself. His movements were jerky, and he realized it was because he felt afraid that if he didn't finish the task quickly enough, she might change her mind.

He carried the mugs into the living room and sat across from her. At first their conversation was awkward, but gradually the tension eased. It amazed him how much they had to talk about. Books, movies, politics. Children. Police work. Life in Alaska. They shared myriad opinions and stories and observations.

It was as though all the difficulties between them had been wiped out and they were starting over.

Mitch laughed. Damn, this felt good. He'd begun to feel warm and relaxed, trusting. Alive. She seemed curious about his past, but her occasional questions were friendly, not intrusive. And she didn't probe for more information than he was willing—or able—to give her.

He brought out a large photo album and sat next to her on the sofa, with the album resting partially on his lap and partially on hers. Mitch turned the pages, explaining each picture.

He wondered what Bethany thought about the gap in his past. It was as if his and Chrissie's life had started when they moved to Hard Luck. There wasn't a single photograph of their lives before the move. Not one picture of Lori.

He turned a page and his hand inadvertently brushed hers. He hadn't meant to touch her, but when he did, it was as if something exploded inside him. For long seconds, neither moved.

Slowly Mitch's gaze sought hers. Instead of accusation, he found approval, instead of anger, acceptance. He released his breath, tired of fighting a battle he couldn't win. With deliberate movements, he closed the photo album and set it aside.

"Mitch?"

"We'll talk later," he whispered. He wrapped his hand around the back of her neck and gently pulled her forward. He needed this. Ached for this.

He kissed her slowly, sweetly, teasing her lips until her head rolled back against the cushion in abject surrender.

"Mitch . . ." She tried once more.

He stopped her from speaking by placing his fingertip against her moist lips. "We both know Chrissie manipulated this meeting."

She frowned as if she was about to question him.

"She's no sicker than you or I."

Bethany blinked.

"Let's humor her."

Her eyes darkened to a deep shade of melted chocolate. "Let's," she agreed, and wound her arms around his neck.

"THANK YOU SO MUCH for coming," Bethany said to Ben. It had taken a lot to convince him to speak to her students.

Ben had resisted, claiming he wasn't comfortable with children, never having had youngsters himself. But in the end Bethany's persistence had won out.

"You did a great job," she told him.

Ben blushed slightly. "I did, didn't I?" He walked about the room and patted the top of each desk as if remembering who had sat where.

"The children loved hearing about your job," she told him. "And about your life in the navy."

"They certainly had lots of questions."

Bethany didn't mention that she'd primed them beforehand. She hadn't had to encourage them much; they were familiar with Ben and fascinated by him.

Bethany wasn't especially proud of the somewhat underhand method she'd used to learn what she could of Ben's past. Still, inviting him to speak to her students was certainly legitimate; he wasn't the only community member she'd asked to do so. Dotty had been in the week before, and Sawyer O'Halloran had agreed to come the week following Thanksgiving. She found herself studying Ben now, looking for hints of her own appearance, her own personality.

"I haven't seen much of you lately," he said, folding his arms. He half sat on one of the desks in the front row. "Used to be you'd stop in once a day, and we'd have a chance for a nice little chat."

"I've been busy lately." In the past week, she'd been seeing a lot of Mitch and Chrissie.

"I kinda miss our talks," Ben muttered.

"Me, too," Bethany admitted. It was becoming increasingly difficult, she discovered, to talk to Ben about personal things. Her fear was that she'd inadvertently reveal their relationship. The temptation to tell him grew stronger with each meeting, something she hadn't considered when she'd decided to find him.

Ben stared at her a moment as if he wasn't sure he should go on. "I thought I saw you with Mitch Harris the other day." It was more question than statement.

She nodded. "He drove me to the library." He'd said he didn't want her walking. The piercing cold continued, but temperatures weren't as low as they'd been earlier in the week. Bethany could easily have trekked the short distance; Mitch's driving her was an excuse—one she'd readily grasped.

"Are you two seeing each other now?"

Bethany hesitated.

"I don't mean to pry," Ben said, studying her. "You can tell me it's none of my damn business if you want, and I won't take offense. It's just that I get customers now and again who're curious about you."

"Like who?"

"Like Bill Landgrin."

"Oh." It embarrassed her no end that she'd had dinner with the pipeline worker. He'd phoned her several times since, and the conversations had always been uncomfortable. Not because of anything Bill said or did, but because she'd dated him for all the wrong reasons.

Bethany walked from behind her desk and over to the blackboard. "I don't know what to tell you about Mitch and me," she said, picking up the eraser.

Ben's face softened with sympathy. "You sound confused."

"I am." Bethany found it easy to understand why people so often shared confidences with Ben; he was a good listener, never meddlesome and always encouraging.

With anyone else, Bethany would have skirted around the subject of her and Mitch, but she felt a strong connection with Ben—one that reached beyond the reasons she'd come to Hard Luck. It wasn't just a connection created by her secret knowledge. Since her arrival, Ben had become her friend. That surprised her; she hadn't expected to like him this much.

"I'm afraid I'm falling in love with Mitch," she said in a soft, breathless voice.

"Afraid?"

She lowered her gaze and nodded. "I don't think he feels the same way about me."

"Why's that?" Ben leaned forward.

"He doesn't *want* to be attracted to me. Every time I feel we're getting close, he backs away. There's a huge part of himself he keeps hidden. He's never discussed Chrissie's mother. I've never really questioned him about her or about his life before he moved to Hard Luck, and he never volunteers."

Ben rubbed one side of his face. "But we all have our secrets, don't you think?"

Bethany nodded and swallowed uncomfortably. She certainly had hers.

"Whatever happened to Mitch cut deep. He lost his wife, the mother of his child. I can tell you because I was living here when Mitch and Chrissie first arrived. Mitch was a wounded soul. Whatever happened, he's kept to himself. He'd been here five years now, and for the first time I've seen him smile. You're good for him and Chrissie. Real good."

"He and Chrissie would be easy to love."

"But you're afraid."

She nodded.

"Seems to me you two've come a long way in a short time. I could be wrong, but not so long ago all you did was send longing looks at each other. Now you're actually talking, spending time together." He paused. "I heard he told Bill Landgrin a thing or two recently."

"Mitch did?"

Ben grinned broadly. "Not in any words I'd care to repeat in front of a lady, mind you. Seems to me he wouldn't have done that if he wasn't serious about you himself. Give him time, Bethany. Yourself, too. You've only been here three months. Rome wasn't built in a day, you know."

Bethany exhaled. "Thank you for listening—and for your advice."

"No problem," Ben said. "It was my pleasure."

Smiling, she closed the distance between them and kissed his rough cheek.

Ben flushed and pressed his hand to his face.

She felt worlds better, and not only because Ben had given her good advice. He'd said the things her own father would have said.

The irony of that thought didn't escape her.

CHAPTER SEVEN

"HI." BETHANY FELT almost shy as she opened her front door to Mitch that Saturday night. Chrissie was so often with them that any time Bethany and Mitch were alone together, an immediate air of intimacy developed between them.

"Hi yourself." Mitch unwound his scarf and took off his protective winter gear. He, too, seemed a little ill at ease.

They looked at each other then quickly glanced away. Anyone watching them would have guessed they were meeting for the first time. Tonight, neither seemed to know what to say, which was absurd, since they often sat and talked for hours about anything and everything.

This newfound need to know each other, as well as the more relaxed tenor of their relationship, came as a result of Thanksgiving dinner with Sawyer and Abbey. The four adults had played cards following dinner. Two couples. It had seemed natural for Bethany to be with Mitch. Natural and right. Conversation had been lively and wide-ranging, and Bethany felt at home with these people. So did Mitch, judging by the way he laughed and smiled. And somehow, whatever he'd been holding inside seemed less important afterward.

They'd all enjoyed the card-playing so much that it had become a weekly event. In the last couple of weeks Bethany had spent a lot of time in Mitch's company, and she believed they'd grown close and comfortable with each other. But then, they were almost always with other people. With Chrissie, of course. With Sawyer and Abbey. The other O'Halloran brothers. Ben. Margaret Simpson. Rarely were they alone. It was this situation that had prompted her to invite him for dinner.

"Dinner's almost ready," she said self-consciously, rubbing her hands on her jeans. "I hope you like Irish stew."

"I love it, but then I'm partial to anything I don't have to cook myself." He smiled and his eyes met hers. He pulled his gaze away, putting an abrupt end to the moment of intimacy.

Bethany had to fight back her disappointment.

"I see you got your Christmas tree," he said, motioning to the scrawny five-foot vinyl fir that stood in the corner of her living room. She would have preferred a live tree, but the cost was astronomical, and so she did what everyone in Hard Luck had done. She ordered a fake tree through the catalog.

"I was hoping you'd help me decorate it," she said. It was only fair, since she'd helped him and Chrissie decorate theirs the night before. Chrissie had chattered excitedly about Susan's slumber party, which was tonight. Bethany wondered if Abbey had arranged the party so Bethany and Mitch would have some time alone together. Whether it was intentional or not, Bethany was grateful.

"Chrissie said the two of you baked cookies today."

"Susan helped, too," she said. Bethany had offered to take both girls for a few hours during the afternoon; Mitch was working, and Abbey wanted a chance to wrap Christmas gifts and address cards undisturbed.

Mitch followed her into the kitchen. They were greeted by the aroma of sage and other herbs. The oven timer went off, and she reached for a mitt to pull out a loaf of crusty French bread.

Mitch looked around. "Is there anything you need me to do?"

"No. Everything's under control." That was true of dinner, perhaps, but little else felt manageable. Mitch suddenly seemed like a stranger, when she thought they'd come so far. It was like the old days—which really weren't so old.

"I'll dish up dinner now," she said.

He didn't offer to help again; perhaps he thought he'd only be in the way. With his hands resting on a chair back, he stood by the kitchen table and waited until she could join him.

The stew was excellent, or so Mitch claimed, but for all the enjoyment she received from it, Bethany could have been eating boot leather. Disappointment settled over her.

"I imagine Abbey's got her hands full," she said, trying to make conversation.

"How many kids are spending the night?" Mitch asked. "Six was the last I heard."

"Seven, if you count Scott."

"My guess is Scott would rather be tarred and feathered than join a bunch of girls to decorate sugar cookies and string popcorn."

"You're probably right." She passed Mitch the bread. He thanked her and took another slice.

Silence.

Bethany didn't know what had happened to the easy camaraderie they'd had over the past few weeks. Each attempt to start a discussion failed; conversation simply refused to flow. The silence grew more awkward by the minute, and finally Bethany could stand it no longer. With her mouth so dry she could barely talk, she threw down her napkin and turned to Mitch.

"What's wrong with us?" she asked.

"Wrong?"

She gulped some water. "We're so blasted *polite* with each other."

"Yeah," Mitch agreed.

"We're barely able to talk."

"I noticed that, too." But he didn't offer any suggestions or solutions.

Bethany met his eyes, hoping he'd do *something* to resolve this dilemma. He didn't. Instead, he set his napkin carefully aside and got to his feet. "I guess I'm not very hungry." He carried his half-full bowl to the sink.

"Oh."

"Do you want me to leave?" he asked.

No! her heart cried, but she didn't say the word. "Do... do you want to go?"

He didn't answer.

Bethany stood up, pressing the tips of her fingers to her forehead. "Stop. Please, just stop. I want to know what's wrong. Did I do something?"

"No. Good heavens, no." He seemed astonished that she'd even asked. "It isn't anything you've done."

Mitch stood on one side of the kitchen and she on the other. "It's my fault," he said in a voice so quiet she could hardly hear him. "You haven't done anything, but—" He stopped abruptly.

"*What?*" she pleaded. "Tell me."

"Listen, Bethany, I think it would be best if I did leave." With that, he walked purposefully into the living room and retrieved his coat from the small entryway closet.

Although the room was warm and cozy, Bethany felt a sudden chill. She crossed her arms as much to ward off the sense of cold as to protect herself from Mitch's words. "It's back to that, is it?" she managed sadly. From the first day in September, Mitch had been running away from her. Every time she felt they'd made progress, something would happen to show her how far they had yet to go.

His hand on the doorknob, he abruptly turned back to face her. When he spoke his voice was hoarse with anger. "I can't be alone with you without wanting to kiss you."

She stared at him in disbelief. "We've kissed before." There had been those memorable passionate kisses. And more recently, affectionate kisses of greeting and farewell. "What's so different now?"

"We're alone."

"Yes, I know." She still didn't understand.

He shook his head, as if it was difficult to continue. "Don't you see, Bethany?"

Obviously she didn't.

"With Chrissie or anyone else around, the temptation is minimized. But when it's just the two of us, I can't think about anything else!" This last part was ground out between clenched teeth. "Don't you realize how much I want to make love to you?"

"Is that so terrible?" she asked quietly.

"Yes." The only sound she could hear was the too-fast beating of her heart. She could see Mitch's pulse hammering in the vein in his neck.

"I can't let it happen," he told her, his back straight, shoulders stiff.

"For your information, making love requires two people," Bethany told him simply. "I wish you'd said something earlier. We could have talked about this... arrived at some understanding. It's true," she added, "the thought of us becoming... intimate has crossed my mind—but I wouldn't have allowed it to happen. At least not yet. It's too soon for either of us."

Without a word, Mitch closed the distance between them. With infinite tenderness he wove his fingers through her hair, and buried his lips against the fragrant skin of her throat. "You tempt me so much."

She sighed and wrapped her arms around him.

"Feeling this way frightens me, Bethany. Overwhelms me."

"We can't run from it, Mitch, or pretend it doesn't exist."

His hands trembled as they slid down the length of her spine, molding her against him. His kiss was slow and melting, and so thorough she was left breathless. She buried her head in his shoulder.

"I guess this means I can put away the celery," she whispered.

"The celery?"

"When the catalog order came, I didn't receive the mistletoe. The slip said it's on back order. I talked to my mom earlier today and told her how disappointed I was— and she suggested celery as a substitute. So I nailed a piece over the doorway. Apparently you didn't notice."

Mitch chuckled hoarsely. "You know what I like best about you?"

"You mean other than my kisses?"

"Yes."

The look in his eyes was as potent as expensive whiskey. "You make me laugh."

The amusement drained from her eyes. "Don't close me out," she said, and her gaze drifted to his lips. "I can't bear it when you shut me out of your life. There isn't anything you can't tell me."

"Don't be so sure." Mitch eased her out of his arms and stared down at her, as if testing the truth of her words. It occurred to her that the expression on his face was like that of a man walking a tightrope over Niagara Falls—not daring to look down and not daring to look back.

"Mitch," she said gently, touching his face, "what is it?"

"Nothing." He turned away. "It's nothing."

Bethany didn't believe that. But she had no choice other than end this discussion, which apparently distressed him so much. When he was ready he'd tell her.

"Didn't you say something about decorating your Christmas tree?" he asked with feigned enthusiasm.

"I did indeed," she said, following his lead.

"Good. We'll get to that in a moment," he said, and took her by the hand.

"Where are we going?"

"You mean you don't know?" He grinned boyishly. "I'm taking you to the celery, er, mistletoe."

Soon she was in his arms, and all the doubts she'd entertained were obliterated the moment he lowered his mouth to hers. She felt only the gentle touch of his lips. Slow and confident. Intimate and familiar.

CHRISTIAN HAD EXPECTED Mariah to move away from Hard Luck before December. He wasn't a betting man, but he would've wagered a year's income that his secretary would high-tail it out of town right after the first snowfall. Not that he'd have blamed her, living as she was in a one-room cabin. He cringed every time he thought about her in those primitive conditions.

It wasn't the first time Mariah had proved him wrong. Christian was convinced she stayed on out of pure spite. She wanted to prove herself, all right, but at the expense of his pride.

He walked into the office to find Mariah already at her desk, typing away at the computer. Her fingers moved so fast they were a blur.

At the sound of the door closing, she looked up—and froze.

"Morning," he said without emotion.

"Good morning," she offered shyly. She glanced away, almost as if she expected him to reprimand her in some way. "The coffee's ready."

"So I see." He wasn't looking forward to this, but someone had to reason with her, and Sawyer had refused to take on the task.

Christian poured himself a cup of coffee, then walked slowly to his desk. "Mariah."

She stared at him with large, frightened eyes. "Did I do something wrong again?"

"No, no," he said quickly, wanting to reassure her. "What makes you think that?" He gave her what he hoped resembled an encouraging smile.

She eyed him as if she wasn't sure she could trust him. "It seems the only time you talk to me is when I've done something wrong."

"Not this time." He sat down at his desk, which wasn't all that far from her own. "It's about you living in the cabin," he said.

He watched her bristle. "I believe we've already discussed this subject," she answered stiffly. "Several times."

"I don't want you there."

"Then you should never have offered the cabins as living accommodations."

"I'd prefer it if you moved in with the other women—in Catherine Fletcher's house," he said, ignoring her comment. Actually having Catherine's house available to them had been a godsend. Two women—Sally and Angie—had moved into the house, and the arrangement was working out well.

The pilots Midnight Sons employed lived in a dorm-size room. It was stark, without much more than a big stove for heating and several bunk beds and lockers, but the men never complained. The house was far more to the women's liking. As soon as it could be arranged they were bringing in two mobile homes for the women.

Until then Christian wasn't comfortable thinking about Mariah—or anyone else—living in a one-room cabin. Not with winter already here.

"I'm just fine where I am," Mariah insisted.

Sawyer thought she was all right there, too, but Christian knew otherwise. At night he lay awake, thinking of Mariah out there on the edge of town in a cabin smaller than a rich man's closet. It had no electric power and no plumbing, and was a far cry from what she'd been accustomed to.

"I'm asking," he said being careful to phrase the words in a way she wouldn't find objectionable, "if you'd move in with Sally and Angie. Just until the spring thaw."

"Why?"

Arguing with her was an exercise in frustration. And the amount of time he wasted fretting over her! That in itself made no sense to him. The fact was, he didn't even *like* Mariah. The woman drove him crazy.

"I'm asking you to move in with them for a reason other than the cabin's primitive conditions." This, of course, wasn't true, but he had to find *some* way of getting her to move. He said the first thing that came to mind.

"I . . . I think one or two of the women are considering leaving Hard Luck. We don't want to lose them."

"Who?"

Christian shrugged. "It's just rumors at this point. But I need someone who can encourage them to stick out the winter. Someone the others like and trust."

She looked at him as if she wasn't sure she should believe him.

"The others need someone they feel comfortable with. They like you, and I think you could help."

Mariah paused. "But I don't believe it's necessary for me to move in with them."

"I do," he answered automatically. "How often do you get a chance to talk with your friends? I can't imagine it's more than once a week." He was stabbing in the dark now.

Mariah nibbled on her lower lip and seemed to be considering his words. "That's true."

"A few aren't having an easy time adjusting to life in the Arctic. Will you do it, Mariah?" he pleaded gently. Heaven knew, he'd tried every other means he could think of to get her to move out of that godforsaken cabin. "Will you move in with the other women?"

She hesitated. "I'll still get the deed to the land and the cabin at the end of the year, won't I?"

"You can have both now." It wasn't the first time he'd made that offer. The sooner she accomplished her goals, he figured, the sooner she'd leave Hard Luck.

"Giving me the title now wouldn't be right. The terms of my contract state that at the end of one year's time I'll be entitled to the cabin and the land. I wouldn't dream of taking the deed a moment sooner."

"Then I'll assure you in writing that the time you spend living with the other women will in no way jeopardize our agreement. You can type up the papers yourself."

He watched her and waited. Waited while the interminable minutes passed. He couldn't believe that one small decision would demand such concentration.

"Will you or won't you?" he demanded when he couldn't stand the silence any longer.

"I will," she said, "but on one condition. I want to talk to the others first and make sure I won't be intruding."

"For the love of heaven," Christian muttered, resisting the urge to bury his face in his hands. "Midnight Sons is paying the rent!"

"I'm well aware of that," Mariah said coolly.

"If I want to move the entire French Foreign Legion into that house, then I'll do it."

"No, you wouldn't," Mariah said with a know-it-all grin. "First, Sawyer wouldn't let you and—"

"It was a figure of speech." Christian now fought the urge to pull out his hair. No one on earth could anger him as quickly as Mariah Douglas. The year she was contracted to work for him couldn't end fast enough. Not until she left Hard Luck would he be able to sleep through the night again.

A WREATH HUNG inside the door of the Hard Luck Café. Flashing miniature lights were strung around the windows. Christmas cards were hung against one wall in a straggling triangle. Bethany guessed the shape was supposed to represent a Christmas tree.

The thank-you notes the children had written following his visit to the classroom were taped against another wall for everyone who came into the café to see. The worn look of those notes told her Ben had read them countless times himself.

"It's beginning to look downright festive around here," Bethany said as she stepped up to the counter.

"Christmas is one of my favorite times of the year," Ben declared. "How about a piece of mincemeat pie to go with your coffee? It's on the house."

"Actually I don't have time for either," Bethany said regretfully. She was on her way to church for choir practice and only had a few minutes. "I came to invite you to my house for Christmas dinner."

Ben's mouth opened and a look of utter astonishment crossed his face. "I'd thought... Me? What about Mitch and Chrissie? Aren't they spending the day with you?"

"I invited them, too. I'm sure I'm not half as good in the kitchen as you, but I should be able to manage turkey and all the goodies that go with it. Besides, it'll do you good to taste someone else's cooking for a change."

He frowned as though this were a weighty decision. "I like my turkey with sage dressing and giblet gravy."

"You got it. My mom always stuffs the bird with sage dressing, and my dad always makes giblet gravy. I wouldn't know how to do it any other way." When he seemed about to refuse, she added, "If you want to contribute something, you can bring one of those mincemeat pies you're trying to fatten me up with."

Ben turned away from her and reached for the rag. He began to wipe the already clean countertop. "I...I don't know what to say." His eyes continued to avoid hers.

"Just say yes. Dinner's at three."

He gestured weakly. "I always keep the place open."

"Close it this year." She almost suggested he should spend the holiday with family, then realized she couldn't. She admitted to herself that she felt close to Ben; she *did* feel that he was family. Perhaps this was emotionally dangerous, but being with him on Christmas Day might help ease the ache of missing her parents.

"Folks generally spend Christmas Day with family," he said. It was as if he'd been able to read her thoughts. "I don't have any left," he told her in a low voice. "At least, none that would want me dropping in unannounced at Christmas."

"I'll be your family, Ben," she offered, waiting for her heart to stop its crazy beating. He had no way of knowing how much truth there was in her words. "And you can be mine. For this one day, anyhow."

"Won't I be in the way? I mean, with you and—"

Bethany reached for his hand and patted it gently. "I wouldn't have invited you if that was the case."

"What about you and Mitch? You two seem to be spending a lot of time together lately—which is good," he hastened to add. "Don't think I've ever seen Mitch look happier, and what I hear folks saying, there's a night-and-day difference with Chrissie. She used to be a shy little thing."

Bethany had the feeling he would have rambled on for an hour if she hadn't stopped him.

"Ben!" She laughed outright. "I'm asking you to Christmas dinner. Will you or won't you come? I need to know how much food to prepare."

She watched his throat work convulsively. "No one ever asked me to Christmas dinner," he said in a strangled voice.

"Well, they are now."

He met her look and his eyes grew suspiciously bright. "What time do you want me there again?"

"Dinner's at three. You come as early as you like, though."

"All right," he said with some difficulty. "I'll be there, and I'll bring one of my pies."

"Good. I'll see you Christmas Day." Having settled that, Bethany left the café.

"Bethany," Ben stopped her. "If you need any help making that gravy, you let me know."

"I will. Thanks for offering."

Not until she was outside, with the cold clawing at her face, did she realize there were tears in her eyes. She quickly brushed them away and hurried on to the church.

CHRISTMAS WAS SUPPOSED to be a joyous time of year. It would be, Matt Caldwell thought, if Karen was with him. He glanced around the Anchorage church. The harder he tried not to think about his ex-wife, the more difficult it became to concentrate on the hymnbook in his hands.

Perhaps it was because the last time he'd been in church was when his grandmother died. The sadness that had taken hold of his heart then hadn't faded in the weeks since.

Matt hadn't made church a habit of late, either. The fact was, he and God weren't on the best of terms. He was quite comfortable ignoring the presence of an almighty being, since evidence of God had been sorely lacking in his life these past few years.

It didn't help that he was once again the only family member who was alone. His parents stood on one side of him, and Lanni and Charles on the other. Those two were so much in love it was painful just being around them.

Although Lanni enjoyed her work with the *Anchorage News,* she hated the long separations from Charles. April couldn't come soon enough as far as she was concerned.

The Christmas Eve church services continued, and the members of the congregation lifted their voices in song. But Matt wasn't in any frame of mind to join in. He'd worked hard during the past three months. Damned hard. Other than his obvious purpose of getting the lodge ready, he'd driven himself in a single-minded effort, but whether it was to impress Karen or to get her out of his system, he no longer knew.

He couldn't help wondering how his ex-wife was spending Christmas. He was pretty confident she wouldn't have a white Christmas in California, though.

Was she alone, the way he was? Did she feel empty inside? Was she thinking of him?

Somehow he doubted it, considering the impetuous way she'd left Alaska. It still bothered him that she hadn't so much as told him she was moving. Instead, she'd contacted his sister, knowing full well that Lanni would tell him.

Once the interminable singing ended, there was the predictable Christmas pageant. Despite his misery, Matt found himself smiling as the Sunday school children gave the performance they'd no doubt been rehearsing for months.

This year, instead of using a doll, they had a newborn infant playing the role of the baby Jesus. This child was anything but meek and mild. In fact, he let out a scream that echoed through the church and started all the children giggling.

Well, that was what they got for using a real baby.

A baby.

His mind froze on the thought. Babies. Children. He glanced around the congregation and noticed a number of families with small children.

Karen had wanted children. They'd had more than one heated discussion on that subject. Matt had been the one against it; he didn't feel ready for fatherhood. Not when his future and career remained unsettled. In retrospect, he could see he'd been right. Dragging a child through a divorce would have been criminal.

Now the likelihood of his having a family was remote at best. He discovered, somewhat to his surprise, that the realization brought with it a new pain. Great. Just what he needed. Another resentment to harbor. Another casualty of his dead marriage. Something else to flail himself with.

He was relieved when the church service ended. At least he hadn't been subjected to a lengthy sermon on top of the singing and the pageant.

Once they were home, his family gathered around the Christmas tree. Traditionally they opened their gifts on Christmas Eve. It had taken some doing for him to dredge up enough spirit to spring for gifts, but he'd managed it.

"How about hot apple cider?" Lanni asked, sitting down next to him.

"Sure," he said, faking a smile. It didn't seem fair to burden everyone else with his misery.

His sister brought him a cup, then sat down next to him. Matt noticed that their mother was busy in the kitchen and his father was talking to Charles.

"I hoped we'd have a minute alone before we get started opening the gifts," Lanni whispered. She searched through the mound of gaily wrapped presents; beneath one of them she found what she was looking for. An envelope. She handed it to him.

Matt looked at his name on the envelope and instantly recognized the handwriting as Karen's. His heart skipped a beat, and he raised his eyes to his sister's, not sure what to think.

"How'd you get this?"

"Karen mailed a gift to me and to Mom and Dad. It was in the same package."

"I see." His hand closed tightly over the envelope.

"There's something else," Lanni said, her gaze avoiding his.

"Yes?" He was eager to escape to his room and read what Karen had written.

"Our wedding..."

"What about it?"

"Would you mind very much if Karen served as my maid of honor?"

Matt stared at his sister, not understanding. "You want her in your wedding party?"

"Yes," she said, then quickly added, "But only if you don't object. I wouldn't want it to be uncomfortable for you, Matt. You're my brother, after all, and she was your wife—but she's still my friend."

"Why should I care?" he mumbled. "It's your wedding." With that, he left the room.

Once he was inside his old bedroom, Matt threw himself onto the bed and tore open the envelope. A single sheet of paper fell from the card. Heart pounding, he unfolded it and read:

Merry Christmas, Matt.
It didn't seem right to mail gifts·to Lanni and your

parents and send you nothing. But at the same time, it's a bit awkward to buy my ex-husband a Christmas gift.

I hope this card finds you well.

Sincerely,
Karen

Sincerely. She'd actually signed the note *sincerely.* Matt couldn't believe it. He picked up the Christmas card he'd discarded earlier and found she'd written nothing but her name.

Well, sending a Christmas card was more than he'd done for her. He supposed he'd have to add that to his long list of failures and regrets.

CHAPTER EIGHT

MITCH WOKE EARLY Christmas morning.

Not wanting to wake Chrissie, he moved silently into the living room, where the miniature lights on the tree glittered like frosted stars. He smiled at their decorations—paper chains, strung popcorn and handmade ornaments.

He rearranged the gifts under the tree. He'd placed them there the night before, after Chrissie had gone to bed. He suspected she didn't believe in Santa Claus any longer, but it was more fun for them both to keep up the pretense.

The largest present wasn't from him, but Bethany. A Barbie thingamajig. Town house or some such nonsense. Only it wasn't nonsense to Chrissie; the kid took her Barbie seriously. She'd be thrilled with this. He knew Chrissie would be happily absorbed with her gifts all morning, and then later, in the afternoon, they were going to Bethany's place for a turkey dinner with all the fixings.

Bethany.

He needed these quiet early-morning moments to clear his thoughts and make sense of his feelings.

It had happened.

Despite his resistance, his best efforts to prevent it, despite his vows to the contrary, despite the full force of his determination, he'd gone and fallen in love with Bethany Ross.

He didn't *want* to love Bethany, and in the same breath, he found himself humbled that this remarkable woman had entered his life. Especially after Lori. Especially now.

Mitch paced the living room, too restless to sit. Admitting that he cared deeply for Bethany required some sort of decision. A man didn't come to this kind of realization without defining a course of action.

He knew he had nothing to offer her. While it was true that he made enough money to support a family, his financial status wasn't impressive enough to mention. Somehow he doubted this would matter much to Bethany, but still...

He was dismally aware, too, that he came to her with deep emotional scars and a needy child in tow. The mere thought of loving again, of trusting again, terrified him. It was enough to cause him to break out in a cold sweat. On top of everything else was the paralyzing fear that he'd fail Bethany the way he had Lori.

Then again, he reminded himself, he had options. He could do what he'd done for these past three months—deny his feelings. Ignore what his heart was telling him.

He might have continued that way for months, possibly years, if it wasn't for one thing.

Chrissie.

From the moment his daughter had met Bethany, she'd set her sights on making the teacher her mother and his wife. Watching the two of them together had touched him from the very first. In ways he'd never fully understand, Bethany ministered to his daughter's need for a mother in the same way she satisfied his own long-repressed desire for a companion. *A wife...*

As the weeks progressed, Chrissie had started looking to Bethany for guidance more and more often. There wasn't *anything* Chrissie wouldn't do to be with her—including feigning flu symptoms.

What confounded him was the fact that Bethany seemed to share his feelings. He felt her love as powerfully as those brief moments of sunlight everyday, brightening the world in the darkness of an Arctic winter.

Admitting his love for Bethany—to her and to himself—wasn't a simple thing. Love rarely was, he suspected. If he told her how he felt about her, he'd also have to tell her about his past.

Love implied trust. And he'd need to trust her with the painful details of his marriage. With that came the tremendous risk of her rejection. He wouldn't blame her if she *did* turn away. If the situation were reversed, he didn't know how he'd react. He was laying an enormous burden on her.

Telling her all this wasn't something he could do on the spur of the moment. Timing was critical. He'd have to wait for the right day, the right mood.

Not this morning, he decided. Not on Christmas. He refused to spoil the day's celebration with the ugliness of his past. No need to darken the holiday with a litany of his failures as a husband.

"Daddy?" Chrissie stood just inside the living-room doorway yawning. She wore her pretty new flannel pajamas—the one gift he'd allowed her to open Christmas Eve.

"Merry Christmas, pumpkin," he said, opening his arms to her. "It looks like Santa made it to Hard Luck safely, after all."

Chrissie leapt into his embrace and he folded his arms around her, slowly closing his eyes. His daughter was the most precious gift he'd ever been given. And now, finding Bethany... His heart was full.

"I CAN'T BELIEVE I ate the whole thing," Ben teased, placing his hands on the bulge of his stomach and sighing heavily. He eased his chair away from the kitchen table. "If anyone else gets wind of what a good cook you are, Bethany, I'll be out of business before I know it."

Bethany smiled, delighted with his praise. "I don't think you have a thing to worry about. Those pies of yours were fabulous, especially the mincemeat. I'd like to get your recipe."

Ben gave her a wide grin. "Sure. No problem. It's one I came up with myself—I like to try new things when I cook. How about you? Have you always been this good in the kitchen?"

It was another trait she shared with her birth father, but once again this wasn't something she could mention.

"Almost always. While other little girls were playing with dolls and makeup, I was using my Betty Crocker Baking Center to concoct pastries and other sugary delights."

"Well, all that practice sure paid off," Mitch said.

Bethany blushed a little at the compliments. She'd done her best to put on a spread worthy of their praise. The meal had taken weeks of careful planning; she'd had to special-order some of the ingredients, and her mother had mailed her the spices. A lot of the dishes she'd made were traditional family recipes. Mashed sweet potatoes with dried apricots and lots of pure, creamery butter. Sage dressing, of course, and another rice-and-raisin dressing that had been a favorite of hers, one her grand-mother made every year.

"You miss your family, don't you?" Mitch asked as he helped her clear the table.

"Everyone does at Christmas, don't you think?" This first year so far away from her parents and two younger brothers had been more difficult than she'd anticipated; this morning had been particularly wrenching. She knew they missed her, too. Bethany had spoken to her family in California at least once a day for the past week. She didn't care how high her phone bill ran.

"I must have chatted to Mom three times this morn-ing alone," she told Mitch. "It's funny. For years I've helped her with Thanksgiving and Christmas dinners, but when it came to doing it on my own, I had a dozen ques-tions."

"You need me to do anything?" Ben asked, getting up from the table. He carried his plate to the sink. "I've done plenty of dishes in my time. I wouldn't mind lend-ing a hand, especially after a meal like that. Seems to me that those who cook shouldn't have to wash the dishes."

"Normally I'd agree with you, but not today. You're my guest."

"But..."

"I should think you'd know better than to argue with a woman," Mitch chided.

Laughing, Bethany shooed Ben out of the kitchen.

"We were going to continue our game of Monopoly, remember?" Chrissie reminded him eagerly. "You said you wanted a chance to win some of your money back."

"Go play," Bethany said with a laugh. "I'll rope Mitch here into helping."

"You're sure?" Ben asked.

"Very sure," she told him, glancing over at Mitch with a gentle smile.

Mitch mumbled something she couldn't hear. She looked at him curiously as she reached for a bowl. "What did you say?"

His eyes held hers. "I said a man could get lost in one of your smiles and never find his way home."

Bethany paused, the bowl of leftover mashed potatoes in her hands. "Why, Mitch, what a romantic thing to say."

His face tightened ever so slightly, as though her comment had embarrassed him. "It must have something to do with the season," he said gruffly. He turned away from her and started to fill the sink with hot, sudsy water.

Bethany smiled to herself. It was a rare thing to see Mitch Harris flustered. Her hand fingered the polished five-dollar gold piece he'd had made into a pendant and placed on a fine gold chain. The coin had been minted the year of her birth, and Mitch had had it mounted in a gold bezel. The necklace was beautiful in its simplicity. The minute she fastened it around her neck, Bethany knew this was a piece of jewelry she'd wear every day for the rest of her life.

She felt that her gift for Mitch paled in comparison. Mitch was an avid Tom Clancy fan, and through a friend who managed a bookstore in San Francisco, she'd been able to get him an autographed copy of Clancy's latest hard cover.

When Mitch had opened the package and read the inscription, he looked up at her as though she'd handed him the stone tablets direct from Mount Sinai.

Chrissie had been excited about her Barbie town house, too.

The one who'd surprised her most, however, was Ben. He'd arrived for dinner with not one pie but four—all of them baked fresh that morning. In addition to the pies, he'd brusquely handed her an oblong box, as though he couldn't be rid of the thing fast enough. Bethany got a kick out of the way he'd wrapped it. He'd used three times the amount of paper necessary and enough tape to supply the U.S. Army for a year.

Inside the box was a piece of scrimshaw made from a walrus tusk. The scene on the polished piece of ivory was of wild geese in flight over a willow-filled marsh. Mountains rose in the distance against a sun-lit sky.

Ben had done his best to dismiss his gift as nothing more than a trinket, but Bethany knew from her brief stay in Fairbanks how expensive such pieces of artwork had become. She tried to thank him, but it was clear her words only served to embarrass him.

"I would have thought you'd want to fly home for Christmas," Mitch said, rolling up the sleeves of his long-sleeved shirt before dipping his hands in the dishwater.

"I thought seriously about it." Bethany wasn't going to minimize the difficulty of her decision to remain in Hard Luck. "But it's a long way to travel for so short a time. I'll probably stay in Alaska during spring break, as well. After all, my commitment here is only for the school year."

"You're going home to California in June, then?"

"Are you asking if I plan to return to Hard Luck for another school year?"

"Yes," he said, his back to her.

Something in the carefully nonchalant way he'd asked told her that her answer was important to him.

"I don't know," she said as straightforwardly as she knew how. "It depends on whether I'm offered a contract."

"And if you are?"

"I...don't know yet." She loved Alaska and her students. Most important of all, she loved Mitch and Chrissie. Ben, too. But there were other factors to consider. Several of them had to do with Ben—should she tell him he was her biological father and what would his reaction be if she did? More and more, she felt inclined to confront him with the truth.

"Well, I hope you come back" was all the response Mitch gave her. The deliberate lack of emotion in his voice was clearly intended to suggest that they'd been talking about something of little importance.

Why, for heaven's sake, couldn't the man just say what he wanted to say?

Hands on her hips, Bethany glared at him. Mitch happened to turn around for another stack of dirty dishes; he saw her and did a double take. "What?" he demanded.

"All you can say is 'Well, I hope you come back,'" she mimicked. "I'm spilling my heart out here and *that's* all the reaction I get from you?"

He gave her a blank look.

"The answer is I'm willing to consider another year's contract, and you can bet it isn't because of the tropical climate in Hard Luck."

Mitch grinned exuberantly. "The benefits are good."

"But not great."

"The money's fabulous."

"Oh, please," she muttered, rolling her eyes. She took an exaggerated breath. "My, my, I wonder what the appeal could be."

Mitch looked at her in sudden and complete seriousness. "I was hoping you'd say it was me."

She regarded him with an equally somber look. "I do enjoy the way you kiss, Mitch Harris."

The first sign of amusement touched his lips. He lifted his soapy arms from the water and stretched them toward her. "Maybe what you need to convince you is a small demonstration of my enjoyable kisses."

A second later Bethany was in his arms. The water seeped through her blouse, but she couldn't have cared less. What *did* matter to her was sharing this important day with the people she loved. And those who loved her.

JOHN HENDERSON wanted to do the right thing by Sally. He loved her—more than he'd thought possible. Proof of that was his willingness to delay asking her to marry him; he was determined to wait until he'd talked to her father.

The engagement ring continued to burn a hole in his pocket. He'd been carrying it with him for weeks now.

Every once in a while he'd draw it out and rub the gold band between his index finger and his thumb. He figured that his patience—difficult though he found it to be patient—was a measure of his love for Sally. Still, he cursed himself a dozen times a day for ever having listened to Duke.

John told himself that the other pilot didn't know any more about love than he did. But it wasn't true; Duke had given him good, sensible advice. John desperately wanted everything to be right between Sally and him, especially after her recent heartbreak.

It would've been selfish to rush her into an engagement and then a wedding without first knowing that she shared his feelings—and was sure of her own. He had to be certain she wasn't marrying him on the rebound. Duke was right about the other thing, too. Sally's family was traditional, old-fashioned, even, and it was important to meet them, to give them a chance to know him. Important—but the waiting had become harder with every week that passed.

Now he was ready to make his move. And ask his questions.

Naturally, John would rather have delayed this initial awkwardness. No man likes to be scrutinized by strangers, especially when he's about to ask these very people for permission to marry the most precious, beautiful woman God ever made. Their daughter.

If he were Sally's father, John thought, he wouldn't blame the man for booting him out of the house. He hoped, however, that it wouldn't come to that.

He'd bought a new suit for the occasion. It wasn't a waste of money, he'd decided, seeing that he'd probably need it for the wedding and all. If Sally agreed to marry him, and he hoped and prayed she would.

Sally's true feelings for him seemed to be the only real question. They'd been seeing each other on a regular basis, but John had noticed certain things about her that left him wondering. Her eyes didn't light up when she saw him, the way they had in the beginning. If he didn't know better, he'd think she was avoiding him lately.

Mariah Douglas had recently moved into the house with her, and Sally seemed almost relieved to have an excuse not to invite him over so often. Of course, he'd been busy at Midnight Sons, with the holiday rush and all.

Other signs baffled him, as well. These puzzling changes in Sally's behavior had started after he'd spent the night with her. It wasn't like he'd *planned* they make love; it had just happened.

A hundred times since, John had regretted not waiting to initiate their lovemaking until after the wedding. He'd known for a long time how he felt about Sally. Immediately following their one night together, he'd gone out and bought the engagement ring, but then Duke had talked him out of proposing until he could meet her family.

It might not be such a good idea to show up unannounced on Christmas Day, but John didn't have a lot of spare time. Midnight Sons was short-handed in the wintertime as it was. The holidays had offered him the opportunity to make the trip. That was why he was in British Columbia, in a small town with an Indian name he couldn't pronounce, dropping in on Sally's family uninvited and clutching a somewhat travel-worn bouquet of roses.

Squaring his shoulders, John checked the address on the back of the Christmas card envelope and walked up to the split-entry white house with the dark green shutters and the large fir wreath on the door. He pressed the doorbell, swallowed nervously and waited.

His relief was great when Sally answered the door herself. Her eyes grew huge with surprise and, he hoped, with happiness when she saw who it was.

"John? What are you doing here?"

He thrust the flowers into her hand, grateful to be rid of them. "I've come to talk to your father," he told her.

"My dad?" she asked, clearly puzzled. "Why?"

"That's between him and me." He found it difficult not to stare at her, seeing she was as pretty as a model for one of those fashion magazines. They'd only made love that once and although he cursed himself for his lack of self-control, he couldn't make himself regret loving Sally. He looked forward to making love to her again. Only this time it would be when his ring was around her finger and they'd said their "I do's."

"John?" She closed the door and stepped onto the small porch steps, hugging her arms around him. Her pretty eyes questioned his. "What's this all about?"

"I need to talk to your father," he repeated.

"You already said that. Is it because I've decided not to return to Hard Luck? Who told you? Not Mariah, she wouldn't do that, I know she wouldn't."

John felt as if someone had punched him. For one shocking moment, he thought he might be sick. "You didn't plan on coming back after Christmas?"

"No." She lowered her gaze, avoiding his.

"But I thought . . . I hoped—" He snapped his mouth shut before he made an even bigger fool of himself. He was about to humble himself before her father and request Sally's hand in marriage. Yet she'd walked out of his life without so much as a word of farewell.

"You mean you didn't know?"

He shook his head. "You weren't planning on telling me?"

"No." She tucked her chin against her chest. "I . . . I couldn't see the point. You'd gotten what you wanted, hadn't you?"

"What the hell is that supposed to mean?" he shouted. Standing outside her family home yelling probably wasn't the best way to introduce himself to her father, but John couldn't help it. He was angry, and with damn good reason.

"You know exactly what I mean," she replied in a furious whisper.

"Are you referring to the night we made love?"

Mortified, Sally closed her eyes. "Do you have to shout it to the entire neighborhood?"

"Yes!"

Sally glared at him. "I think we've said everything there is to say to each other."

"Not by a long shot, we haven't," John countered. "Okay, so we made love. Big deal. I'm not perfect, and neither are you. It happened, but we haven't gone to bed since then, have we?"

"John, please, not so loud." Sally glanced uneasily over her shoulder.

His next words surprised him, springing out despite himself. "I wasn't the first, so I don't understand why you're making a federal case over it. Too late now, anyway." He would never have said this if he hadn't been so angry, so much in pain.

Tears instantly leapt into her eyes and John would have given his right arm to take back the hurtful words. He'd rather suffer untold tortures than say anything to distress Sally, yet he'd done exactly that.

The door behind her opened and a burly lumberjack of a man walked out onto the porch. "What's going on here?"

Sally gestured weakly toward John. "Daddy, this is John Henderson. He—he's a friend from Hard Luck."

Finding his daughter sniffling back tears wasn't much of an endorsement, John thought gloomily. He squared his shoulders and offered the other man his hand. "I'm pleased to meet you, Mr. McDonald."

"The name's Jack. I don't understand why my daughter hasn't seen fit to invite you into the house, young man." He cast an accusatory glance in Sally's direction. "Seems you've come a long way to visit my daughter."

"It doesn't look like I was as welcome as I thought I'd be," John muttered.

"Nonsense. It's Christmas Day. Since you've traveled all this way, the least we can do is ask you to join us and offer you a warm drink."

John didn't need anything to warm him. Spending time with the McDonald family would only add to his frustration and misery, but Jack McDonald gave him no option. Sally's father quickly ushered him inside.

Swallowing his pride, John followed the brawny man up a short flight of stairs and into the living room. The festivities ceased when he appeared. Sally's father introduced him around, and her mother poured him a cup of wassail that tasted like hot apple cider.

"I don't believe Sally's mentioned you in her letters home," Mrs. McDonald said conversationally as a chair was brought out for John.

He felt his heart grow cold and heavy with pain. Forcing himself to observe basic good manners, he thanked Sally's brother for the chair. All those months while he was pining over Sally, he hadn't managed to rate a single line in one of her letters home. Although he'd told her their making love had been no big deal, it *had* been. For him. He loved her. But apparently their relationship wasn't important enough to Sally to ever tell her his name.

"I told you about John," Sally said weakly.

John wondered if that was true, or if she was attempting to cover her tracks.

"John's the bush pilot I wrote you about." Sally sat across the room from him and tucked her hands awkwardly between her knees as if she wasn't sure what to do with them.

"Oh yes, now I remember. Don't think you mentioned his name, though." Her father nodded slowly. And her mother gave him a sudden, bright smile.

John drank down the cider as fast as his throat would accept it. It burned going down, but he didn't care. He drained the cup, stood and abruptly handed it to Sally's mother.

"Thank you for the drink and the hospitality, but I need to be on my way."

Jack bent down to the carpet and retrieved something. "I believe you dropped this, son," he said.

To John's mortification, Sally's father held out the engagement ring.

He checked his pocket, praying all the while that there were two such rings in this world, and that the second just happened to be in Sally's home. On the floor. Naturally, the diamond Jack held was the one he'd brought for Sally. Without a word, he slipped it back inside his suit pocket.

"It was a pleasure meeting everyone," he said, anxiously eyeing the front door. He'd never been so eager to leave a place. Leave and find somewhere to be by himself.

Well, he told himself bitterly, he'd learned his lesson when it came to women. He was better off living his life alone. To think he'd been one of the men eager to have the O'Hallorans bring women north!

One thing was certain, he didn't need this kind of rejection, this kind of pain.

"John?" Sally gazed at him with those big, beautiful blue eyes of hers. Only this time he wasn't about to be taken in by her sweetness.

He ignored her and hurried down the stairs to the front door. He'd already grasped the door handle when he realized that Sally had followed him. "You can leave without explaining that ring, but I swear if you do I'll never speak to you again."

"I don't see that it'd matter," he told her, boldly meeting her eyes. "You weren't planning on speaking to me anyway."

He gave her ample time to answer, and when she didn't, he made a show of turning the knob.

"Don't go," Sally cried in a choked whisper. "I thought . . . that you'd gotten what you wanted and so you—"

"I know what you thought," he snapped.

"Maybe we could talk this out?" It sounded like she was struggling not to break into tears. Damn, but she knew he couldn't bear to see her cry. He dug inside his back pocket, pulling out a fresh handkerchief and handing it to her.

"Could we talk, John?" she asked and walked down the second flight of stairs to the lower portion of the house. "Please?"

John guessed he was supposed to follow her. He looked up to find her mother, father, brother and a few cousins whose names he'd forgotten leaning over the railing staring at him.

"You'd better go," Sally's younger brother advised, "it's best to do what she wants when she's in one of these moods."

"Do you love her, son?" Jack McDonald demanded.

John looked at Sally, thinking a response now would be premature, but he couldn't very well deny it, carrying an engagement ring in his pocket. "Yes, sir. I meant to ask Sally to marry me, but I wanted everything to be right with us. I thought I'd introduce myself and ask your permission first."

"It's a good man who speaks to the father first," Sally's mother said, nodding tearfully.

"Marry her with my blessing, son."

John relaxed and grinned. "Thank you, sir." Then he figured he'd better give himself some room in case things didn't go the way he hoped. "In light of what's happened, I'm not sure Sally will say yes. She wasn't planning on returning to Hard Luck—I'm not sure why, but she hadn't said a word about it to me."

"I believe my daughter's about to clear away any doubts you have, young man. She'll give you plenty of reasons not to change your mind."

"Daddy!" This drifted up from the bottom of the stairwell.

John winked at his future in-laws. "That's what I was hoping she'd do," he said and hurried down the stairs, his steps jubilant. "Oh, and Merry Christmas, everyone!"

CHAPTER NINE

IT SHOULDN'T UPSET HER. If anything, Bethany thought, she should be pleased that Randy Kincade was getting married. The invitation for the March wedding arrived the second week of January, when winter howled outside her window and the promise of spring was buried beneath the frozen ground.

Bethany wasn't generally prone to bouts of the blues. But the darkness and the constant cold nibbled away at her optimism. Cabin fever—she'd never experienced it before, but she recognized the symptoms.

Her hair needed a trim, and she longed to see a movie in a real theater that sold hot, buttered popcorn. It was the middle of January, and she'd have killed for a thick-crust pizza smothered in melted cheese and chunks of spicy Italian sausage.

The craving for a pizza brought on a deluge of other sudden, unanticipated wants. She yearned for the opportunity to shop in a mall, in stores with fitting rooms, and to stroll past kiosks that sold delights like long, dangling earrings and glittery T-shirts. Not that she'd buy a lot of items. She just wanted to *see* them.

To make everything even worse, her relationship with Mitch had apparently ground to a standstill. As each week passed, it became more and more obvious that her feelings for him were far stronger than his were for her.

Whimsically she wondered if this was because God wanted her to know how Randy must have felt all those years ago when she didn't return the fervor of his love.

So now she knew, and it hurt like hell.

Not that Mitch had said anything. Not directly at least. It was his manner, his new reserve, the way he kissed her—as if even then he felt the need to protect his heart.

It frustrated Bethany. It angered her, but mostly it hurt. In many ways, she felt their relationship had become more honest and open, yet in others—the important ones—he still seemed to be holding back. He seemed to fear that loving her would mean surrendering a piece of his soul, and she'd begun to wonder if he'd always keep the past hidden from her.

On another front, she increasingly felt an urge to let Ben know she was his daughter. Perhaps this was because she missed her family so much. Or maybe it was because she'd come to terms with Ben's place in her life. Then again, maybe it was because she felt frustrated in her relationship with Mitch. She didn't know.

This wasn't to say the soulful kisses they shared weren't wonderful. They were. Yet they often left her hungering, not for a deeper physical relationship, but for a more profound emotional one. She longed for Mitch to trust her with his past, and clearly he wasn't willing to do that.

Their times alone, she noted, seemed to dwindle instead of increase. It almost seemed as though Mitch encouraged Chrissie's presence to avoid being alone with Bethany. It almost seemed as though dating Bethany satisfied his daughter's needs, but not his own.

On this January Saturday evening, when Bethany joined Mitch and Chrissie for their weekly video night, she couldn't disguise her melancholy. She tried, she honestly tried, to be upbeat, but it had been a long-drawn-out week. And now Randy was engaged, while her own love life had stalled.

Mitch must have noticed she hadn't touched the popcorn he'd supplied. "Is something wrong?" he asked, shifting in his seat beside her on the couch.

"No," she whispered, fighting to hold back the emotion that bubbled up inside her, seeking escape. Tears burned for release, and she feared she was about to weep and could think of no explanation that would appease him. No explanation, in fact, that would even make sense.

Mitch and Chrissie glanced at each other, then at her. Mitch stopped the movie. "You look like you're about to cry. I understand this movie's a tearjerker, but I didn't expect you to start crying while the previews were still playing."

She smiled weakly at his joke. "I'm sorry," she said. Her throat closed up, and when she tried to speak again, her voice came out in a high-pitched squeak.

"Bethany, what's wrong?"

She got to her feet, then didn't know why she had. She certainly didn't have anything to say, nor did she know what to do.

"I—I need a haircut," she croaked.

Mitch looked to Chrissie, as if his daughter should be able to translate that. Chrissie regarded Bethany seriously, then shrugged.

"And a pizza—not the frozen kind, but one that's delivered, and the delivery boy should stand around until he gets a tip and act slightly insulted by how little it is." She attempted a laugh, but that failed miserably.

"Pizza? Insulted?" Her explanation, such as it was, seemed to confuse Mitch even more.

"I'm sorry," she said again, gesturing forlornly with her hands. "I really am." She tucked her fingers against her palms and studied her hands. "Look at my nails. Just look. They used to be long and pretty—now they're broken and chipped."

"Bethany—"

"I'm not finished," she said, brushing the tears from her face. Now that they'd started, she couldn't seem to stop them. "I feel like the walls are closing in on me. I need more than a couple of hours of light a day. I'm sick and tired of watching the sun set two hours after dawn. I need more *light* than this." Even though she knew she wasn't being logical, Bethany couldn't stop the words any more than she could the tears. "I want to buy a new bra without ordering it out of a catalog."

"What you're feeling is cabin fever," Mitch explained calmly.

"I *know* that, but . . ."

"We all experience it in one way or another. It's not uncommon in winter. Even those of us who've lived here for years go through this.

"What you need is a weekend jaunt into Fairbanks. Two days away will make you feel like a new woman."

Men always seemed to have a simple solution to everything. For no reason she could explain—after all, she *wanted* to visit a big city—Mitch's answer only irritated her.

"Is a weekend trip going to change the fact that Randy's getting married?" she argued. Her hands clenched into fists, and her arms hung stiffly at her sides.

It took Mitch a moment or so to ask, "Who's Randy?"

"Bethany was engaged to him once a long time ago," Chrissie supplied.

"Do you love him?" Mitch asked in a gentle tone.

His tenderness, his complete lack of jealousy, infuriated her beyond reason. "No," she cried, "I love you, you idiot! Not that you care or notice or anything else." Convinced she'd made an even bigger fool of herself, Bethany reached for her coat and hat.

"Bethany—"

"You don't understand *any* of what I'm feeling, do you? Please, just leave me alone."

To add insult to injury, Mitch stepped back and did precisely as she asked.

By the time Bethany had walked home—having refused Mitch's offer of a ride—she was sobbing openly. Tears had frozen to her face. The worst part was that she *knew* how ridiculous she was being. Unfortunately it didn't seem to matter.

She was weeping uncontrollably—and all because she couldn't have a pizza delivered. Mitch seemed to think all she needed was a weekend in Fairbanks. It didn't escape her notice that he didn't suggest the two of them fly in together.

"Fairbanks, my foot," she muttered under her breath.

Restless and discontented, Bethany found she couldn't bear to sit around the house and do nothing. She was lonely and heartbroken. This type of misery preyed on itself, she realized. What she needed was some kind of distraction. And some sympathy...

Then, on impulse, she phoned Mariah Douglas, who was living in Catherine Fletcher's house now. She hoped she could talk Mariah into inviting her over. Mariah sounded pleased to hear from her and even said she had a bottle of wine in the fridge.

Before long, the two sat in the living room, clutching large glasses of zinfandel and bemoaning their sorry fate.

It seemed the secretary of Midnight Sons shared Bethany's melancholy mood. Not long afterward, Sally McDonald and Angie Hughes, Mariah's housemates, showed up and willingly raided their own stashes of wine and potato chips.

Bethany acknowledged that it felt good to talk with female friends, to compare her list of woes with others who appreciated their seriousness. Soon it wasn't the lack of a decent pizza they were complaining about, but a more serious problem: the men in their lives.

"He wants me gone, you know," Mariah said, staring into her wineglass with a woebegone look. "He takes every opportunity to urge me to leave Hard Luck. I don't think August will come soon enough for him. I've...tried to be a good secretary, but he flusters me so."

Bethany knew Mariah was referring to Christian O'Halloran and wondered what prompted the secretary to stay when her employer had made his views so plain.

Then Bethany realized that Mariah stayed for the same reasons she did.

Bethany swirled the wine in her goblet. Her head swam, and she realized she was already half-drunk. A single glass of wine and she was tipsy. That said a lot about her social life.

"Let's go to Fairbanks!" she suggested excitedly. Although she'd rejected Mitch's suggestion out of hand, it held some appeal now. Escape by any means available was tempting, especially after a sufficient amount of wine.

"You want to leave for Fairbanks now?" Mariah asked incredulously.

"Why not?" Sally McDonald asked. Of them all, Sally was the one with least to complain about—at least on the male front. Sally and John Henderson had become engaged over the Christmas holidays.

"I don't fly. Do you?" Mariah asked. They looked at each other, then broke into giggles.

"I don't fly," Bethany admitted. "But we aren't going to let a little thing like a lack of a pilot stop us, are we? Not when we live in a town chock-full of them."

"You're absolutely right." Mariah's eyes lit up and she wagged her index finger back and forth. "Duke'll do it. He's scheduled for the mail run first thing in the morning and we'll tag along. Now, which of you girls is coming? No, *are* coming. No..."

There were no other volunteers. "Then it's just Beth and me. No, Beth and *I*..."

It was at this point that Bethany realized her friend was as tipsy as she was herself. "How will we get back?"

"I don't know," Mariah said, enunciating very carefully. "But where there's a way there's a will."

Bethany shut her eyes. That didn't sound exactly right, but it was close enough to satisfy her. Especially when she was half-drunk and her heart dangled precariously from her sleeve.

"He doesn't love me, you know," she said, making her own confession.

"Mitch?"

It was time to own up to the truth, however painful.

"He cares for you, though." This came from Sally.

Bethany fingered the gold coin that hung from the delicate chain around her neck. The gift Mitch had given her for Christmas. Touching it now, she experienced a deep sense of loss.

"Mitch does care," she agreed in a broken voice, "but not enough."

Mariah looked at her with sympathy and asked with forced cheer, "Who wants to go to Ben's? A few laughs, a dance or two..."

MITCH LOST COUNT of the number of times he'd tried to reach Bethany by phone. He'd left Chrissie with a high school girl who lived next door and walked over to Bethany's house. He stood on the tiny porch and pounded on the door until his fist hurt, despite the padding provided by his thick gloves.

Clearly she wasn't home. He frowned, wondering where she could possibly have gone.

Even as he asked the question, he knew. She'd gone to Ben's. Folks tended to let their hair down a bit on Fridays and Saturdays.

It wasn't uncommon to find Duke and John lingering over a cribbage board, while the other pilots shot the breeze over nothing in particular. Every now and again, one or more of the pipeline workers would wander in on their way to Fairbanks for a few days of R and R. Things occasionally got a bit rowdy; Mitch had broken up more than one fight in his time. He didn't like the idea of Bethany getting caught in the middle of anything like that.

When he stepped into the Hard Luck Café, he found the noise level almost painful. He couldn't recall the last time he'd seen the place so busy. It was literally hopping.

He caught sight of Bethany dancing with Duke Porter. Mariah Douglas was dancing with Keith Campbell, a pipeline employee and a friend of Bill Landgrin's. Mitch didn't trust either man.

Christian O'Halloran sat brooding in the corner, nursing a drink. Mitch noted that he was keeping a close eye on Mariah. Mitch suspected she wouldn't tolerate or appreciate Christian's interference and that Keith knew it and used it to his advantage.

Frowning, Mitch made his way into the room. He wanted to talk to Bethany, reason with her if he could. He understood her complaints far better than she realized. Her accusations had hit him like a . . . like a fist flying straight through time. Those were the words Lori had said to him day after day, week after week, month after month. . . .

Before he'd realized that it was Bethany talking to him and not his dead wife, Bethany had left. He needed to explain to her that he *did* know what she was experiencing. He'd been through it himself.

In January when daylight was counted in minutes, instead of hours, it did feel as though the walls were closing in.

He wanted to sit down and talk to her and say what had been burdening his heart for weeks now. Since Christmas. *He loved her.* So much it terrified him. He wanted to tell her about Lori; he hadn't, simply because he was afraid of her response. Most of all, he wanted to tell her he loved her.

Bill Landgrin saw him, and the two eyed each other malevolently. From the looks of it, Bill was more than a little put out over their last meeting. From the gleam in his eyes, he'd welcome a confrontation with Mitch.

Mitch wasn't eager for a fight, but he wouldn't back away from one, either.

Bill's gaze traveled from Mitch to Bethany and then back again. He set his mug on the counter and made his way to the other side of the café, where Bethany was sitting, now that her dance with Duke was over. Mitch started in her direction himself, scooting around tables.

Bill beat him to the punch.

"Beth, sweetheart." Mitch heard the other man greet her. "How's about a dance?"

It seemed to Mitch that she was about to refuse, but he made the mistake—a mistake he recognized almost immediately—of answering for her.

"Bethany's with me," he said, his words as cold as the Arctic ice.

"I am?" she asked.

"She is?" Bill echoed. He rubbed his forehead as though to suggest he found it hard to believe Bethany would align herself with the likes of Mitch. "Seems to me the lady's intelligent enough to make her own decisions."

It took Bethany an eternity to make up her mind. "I don't imagine one dance would hurt," she finally said to Bill.

Mitch's jaw hardened. He didn't blame her for defying him; he'd brought it on himself. Somehow the fact that she'd dance with another man, for whatever reason, didn't sit right with him. Not when she'd said she loved him!

He sat down in the chair she'd vacated, and as he watched Bill draw Bethany into his arms, his temperature rose. He wasn't a drinking man, but he sure could have used a shot of something strong right about then.

The song seemed to drone on for a lifetime. When he couldn't bear to sit any longer, Mitch got to his feet and restlessly prowled the edges of the dance area. Not once did he let his eyes waver from Bethany and Bill.

Something that gave him reason to rejoice was the fact that she didn't seem to be enjoying herself. Her gaze found his over Landgrin's shoulder, and she bit her lower lip in a way that told him she was sorry she'd ever agreed to this.

He resisted the urge to cut in.

Although Bethany was in another man's arms, Mitch found himself close to laughter. She'd said she loved him and in the same breath had called him an idiot. He was beginning to suspect she was right. He *was* an idiot. Love seemed to reduce him to that.

The music finally ended, and as Landgrin escorted Bethany to her table and reluctantly left her there, the tension eased from Mitch's body.

He made a beeline for her, regretting now that he hadn't been waiting for her when she returned. But he didn't want to give her reason to think he didn't trust her.

Unfortunately Keith Campbell reached her before he did. "A dance, fair lady?" Keith asked, bowing from the waist.

Again Mitch was left cooling his heels while Bethany frolicked across the dance floor in the arms of yet another man. While he waited, he ordered a soda and checked his watch.

He'd told Diane Hestead, the high school girl staying with Chrissie, that he wouldn't be more than an hour or so. He'd already been gone that long, and it didn't look like he'd be back home any time soon.

With the music blaring, he found the phone and made a quick call to tell Diane he'd be longer than expected.

"Bethany certainly seems to be have captured a few hearts, hasn't she?" Ben commented, slapping Mitch good-naturedly on the back.

"I don't know why she needs to do that," he grumbled. "She's had mine for weeks."

"Does she know that?" Ben asked.

"No," Mitch blurted.

"What do you expect her to do, then?"

Ben was right, of course. Mitch returned to the table to wait for her. When the dance finished, he made damn certain he was there. "My turn," he announced flatly the minute the two of them were alone.

Bethany's gaze narrowed; she promptly ignored him and sat down. She finished the last of her soda and set the glass aside.

"Let's dance," he said, and held out his hand to her.

"Is that a request or a command?" she asked, staring up at him.

Mitch swallowed. This was going from bad to worse. "Do you want me to put on a little performance for you the way Keith did?"

"No," she answered simply.

It was now or never. "Bethany," he said, dragging air into his oxygen-starved lungs, "I love you. I have for weeks. I should have told you before now."

She stared at him, her eyes huge and round. Then, as though she found reason to doubt his words, she hastily looked away. "Why now, Mitch?"

He could hardly hear her over the music. "Why now what?"

"Why are you telling me now?" she asked, clarifying her question. "Is it because you're overwhelmed by the depth of your feelings?" She sounded just a little sarcastic, he thought. "Or could the truth be that you can't bear to see me with another man?"

He frowned, not because he didn't understand her question, but because he wasn't sure how to answer. Certainly she had a point. He might well have been content to leave matters as they were if he hadn't found her dancing with Landgrin.

"Your hesitation tells me everything I need to know," she whispered brokenly. She stood then, in such a rush that she nearly toppled the chair. "Duke," she called, hurrying toward the pilot. "Didn't I promise you another dance?"

Mitch ground his teeth in frustration.

He'd started toward the door when Bill Landgrin stopped him. "Looks like you're batting zero, old friend. Seems to me the lady knows what she wants, and it isn't you."

"I BLEW IT," Bethany muttered miserably. She'd lingered behind and was helping Ben clear the last remaining tables. Mariah had disappeared hours earlier after a confrontation with Christian, and she hadn't seen her friend since.

"What do you mean?"

"Mitch and me."

"What's with you two, anyway?" Ben asked as he set a tray of dirty glasses on the counter.

"I don't know anymore. I thought... I'd hoped..." She felt tongue-tied, unable to explain. Slipping onto the stool opposite Ben, she let her shoulders sag in abject misery. She was still feeling a little drunk and a lot discouraged—not to mention suffering from a near-fatal bout of cabin fever.

"Here," Ben said, reaching behind the counter and bringing out a bottle of brandy. "I save this for special occasions."

"What's so special about this evening?" she asked.

"A number of things," he said, but didn't elaborate. He brought out a couple of snifters and poured a liberal amount into each one. "This will cure what ails you. Guaranteed."

"Maybe you're right." At this point she figured a glass of brandy couldn't hurt.

"Cheers," Ben said, and touched the rim of his glass to hers.

"To a special . . . friend," she said and took her first tentative sip. The liquid fire glided over her tongue and down her throat. When it came to drinking alcohol, Bethany generally stuck to wine and an occasional beer, rarely anything stronger.

Her eyes watered, and this time it had nothing to do with her emotions.

"You all right?" Ben asked, slapping her on the back.

She pressed her hand over her heart and nodded breathlessly. She found her second and third sips went down far more easily than the first. Gradually a warmth spread out from the pit of her stomach, and a lethargic feeling settled over her.

"Have you ever been in love?" she asked, surprising herself by asking such a personal question. Perhaps the liquor had loosened her tongue; more likely it was simply the need to hear this man's version of his affair with her mother. This man who'd fathered her. . . .

"In love? Me?"

"What's so strange about that?" she asked lightly, careful not to let on how serious the question really was. "Surely you've been in love at least once in your life. A woman in your deep, dark past maybe—one you've never been able to forget?"

Ben hesitated, then chuckled. "I was in the navy, you know?"

Bethany nodded. "Don't tell me you were the kind of sailor who had a woman in every port?"

He grinned almost boyishly and cocked his head to one side. "That was me, all right."

Although she'd solicited it, this information disturbed Bethany. It somehow cheapened her mother and the love she'd once felt for Ben. "But surely there was one woman you remember more than any of the others," she pressed.

Ben scratched the side of his head as though to give her question heavy-duty consideration. "Nope, can't say there was. I was the kind who liked to play the field."

Bethany took another sip of the brandy. "What about Marilyn?" she asked brazenly, tossing caution to the winds. "You do remember her, don't you?"

"Marilyn?" Ben repeated, surprise in his eyes. "No...I don't recall any Marilyn." He sounded as though he'd never heard the name before.

Ben might as well have reached across the counter and slapped her face. Hard. She hurt for her mother, and for herself. Before she met him, she'd let herself imagine that her mother's affair with Ben had been a romantic relationship gone tragically awry.

In the past few weeks, she'd began to think she shared a special friendship with Ben. A real bond. Because of that, she'd lowered her guard and come close to revealing her secret.

Bethany clamped her mouth shut. She wanted to blame the wine. The brandy. Both had loosened her tongue, she realized, but she'd been on the verge of telling him, anyway. She brushed the hair out of her face and looked past him.

"Three years ago," she began resolutely, struggling to find the right words, knowing she couldn't stop now, "the doctors found a lump in my mother's breast."

"Cancer?"

Bethany nodded.

Ben glanced at his watch. "It's getting kind of late, don't you think?"

"This story will only take a couple more minutes," she promised, and to fortify her courage, she drank the rest of the brandy in a single gulp. It raged a slick, fiery path down her throat.

"You were talking about your mother," Ben prodded, and it seemed he wanted her to hurry. Bethany didn't know if she could. Those weeks when her mother had been so sick from the chemotherapy had been the most traumatic of her life.

"It turned out that the cancer had spread," Bethany continued. "For a while we didn't know if my mother was going to survive. I was convinced that if the cancer didn't kill her, the chemotherapy would. I was still in college at the time. My classes let out around two, and I got into the habit of stopping off at the hospital on my way home from school."

Ben nursed his drink, his eyes avoiding hers.

"One day, after a particularly violent reaction to the treatment, Mom was convinced she was going to die. I tried to tell her she had to fight the cancer."

"Did she die?" Ben asked. For the first time since starting her story she had his full attention. Either she was a better storyteller than she realized, or Ben did remember her mother.

"No. She's a survivor. But that day Mom asked me to sit down because she had something important to tell me." At this point, Bethany paused long enough to steady herself. After all this time, the unexpectedness of her mother's announcement still shocked her.

"And?"

"My mother told me about a young sailor she'd once loved many years ago. They'd met the summer before he shipped out to Vietnam. By the end of their time together, they'd became lovers. Their political differences separated them as much as the war had. He left because it was his duty to fight, and she stayed behind and joined the peace movement, protesting the war every chance she had. She wrote him a letter and told him about it. He didn't answer. She knew he didn't approve of what she was doing."

"Whoever this person was, he probably didn't want to read about what she was doing to undermine his efforts in Southeast Asia, don't you think?" Ben asked stiffly.

"I'm sure that's true," Bethany said, and her voice vacillated slightly. "The problem was that when he refused to open her next letter, he failed to learn something vitally important. My mother was pregnant with his child."

The snifter in Ben's hand dropped to the floor and shattered. His eyes remained frozen on Bethany's face.

"I was that child."

The silence stretched taut to the breaking point. "Who took care of her?" he asked in a choked whisper.

"Her family. When she was about four months pregnant, she met Peter Ross, another student, and she confided in him. They fell in love and were married shortly before I was born. Peter raised me as his own and has loved and nurtured me ever since. I never would have guessed . . . It was the biggest shock of my life to learn he wasn't my biological father."

"Your mother's name is Marilyn?"

"Yes, and she named you as my birth father."

"Me," Ben said with a weak-sounding laugh. "Sorry, kid, but you've got the wrong guy." He continued to shake his head incredulously. "What'd your mother do— send you out to find me?"

"No. Neither of my parents know the reason I accepted the teaching contract in Hard Luck. I gave your name to the Red Cross, and they traced you here. I came to meet you, to find out what I could about you."

"Then it's unfortunate you came all this way for nothing," he said gruffly.

"It's funny, really, because we *are* alike. You know the way you get three lines between your eyes when you're troubled or confused? I get those, too. In fact you're the one who mentioned it, remember? And we both like to cook. And we—"

"That's enough," he snapped. "Listen, Bethany, this is all well and good, but like I already said, you've got the wrong guy."

"But—"

"I told you before and I'll tell again. I never knew any woman by the name of Marilyn. You'd think if I'd slept with her, I'd remember her, wouldn't you?"

His words were like stones hurled at her heart. "I don't want anything from you, Ben."

"Well, don't count on a mention in my will, either, understand?"

She nearly fell off the stool in her effort to escape. She retreated a step backward. "I...I should never have told you."

"I don't know why you did. And listen, I'd appreciate it if you didn't go spreading this lie around town, either. I've got a reputation to uphold, and I don't want your lies—and your mother's—besmirching my character."

Bethany thought she was going to be sick.

"It's a damn lie, you hear? It's a lie!" This last part was shouted at her.

"I'm sorry. I shouldn't have said anything."

He didn't answer her right away. "I don't know anything about any Marilyn."

"I made a mistake," Bethany whispered. "A terrible mistake." She turned and ran from the café.

CHAPTER TEN

IN ALL THE YEARS Mitch had lived in Hard Luck, he'd seen very few mornings when Ben wasn't open for business.

Mitch wasn't the only disgruntled one. Christian met him outside the café. "Do you think Ben might have overslept?"

Mitch doubted it. "Ben?" he asked. "Ben Hamilton, who says he never sleeps past six no matter what time he goes to bed?"

"Maybe he decided to take the day off. He's entitled, don't you think?" Christian asked.

Mitch had thought of that, too. "But wouldn't he put up a sign or something?"

Christian considered this, then said, "Probably." He checked his watch. "Listen, I'm supposed to meet Sawyer at his place."

"Go ahead." It was clear Christian was thinking the same thing as Mitch. Something was wrong. "I'll check things out and connect with you later," he promised.

Ben's apartment was situated above the café. Mitch had never been inside, and he didn't know anyone who had. Ben's real home was the café itself. He kept it open seven days a week and most holidays. Occasionally he'd post a closed sign when he felt like taking off for a few days' fishing, but that was about it.

The Hard Luck Café was the social center of town, the one place where people routinely gathered. Ben was part psychologist, part judge, part confidant and all friend. Mitch didn't know a man, woman or child in town who didn't like him.

Frowning, and growing increasingly worried, Mitch went around to the back door that led to the kitchen. After a couple of tentative knocks, he walked into the dark, silent café. Flicking on the light switch, the first thing Mitch noticed was shattered glass on the floor.

"Ben!" Mitch called out, walking all the way into the café.

Nothing.

The door to the stairs leading to Ben's apartment was open, and Mitch started up, his heart pounding in his ears. In an effort to compose himself, he paused halfway, fearing what he might find. If Ben was dead, it wouldn't be the first time he'd come upon a body. The last time had been when he'd found Lori.

He broke out in a cold sweat, and his breathing grew shallow. "Ben," he said again, not as loudly this time. It was another moment before he could continue upward.

The apartment itself was ordinary. A couch and television constituted the living room furniture. Small bath. Bedroom. Both doors had been left ajar.

"Ben?" he tried once more.

A moan came from the bedroom.

More relieved than words could express, Mitch hurried into the room. Ben was sprawled across the top of the bedspread. It took him a full minute to sit up. He blinked as if the act of opening his eyes had pained him.

"Are you all right?" Mitch asked.

Ben rubbed a hand down his face and seemed to give the question some consideration. "No," he finally said.

"Do you need me to call Dotty? Or take you to the clinic?"

"Hell, no. She can't do anything about a hangover."

"You're hung over?" To the best of his knowledge, Ben rarely drank.

Ben pressed both hands to his head. "Do you have to talk so blasted loud?" He grimaced at the sound of his own voice.

"Sorry," Mitch said in an amused whisper.

"Make yourself useful, would you?" Ben growled. "I need coffee. Make it strong, too. I'll be downstairs in a few minutes."

Mitch had the coffee brewing and had swept up the broken glass by the time Ben appeared, his eyes red-rimmed and clouded. His gaze shifted toward Mitch before he claimed a stool at the counter.

Mitch brought him a cup of coffee the minute it finished brewing.

"Thanks," Ben mumbled.

"I've never known you to get drunk," Mitch said conversationally, curious as to what had prompted Ben's apparent binge.

"First time in ten years or more," he muttered. "It was either that or... hell, I don't know what. There didn't seem to be a whole lot of options. Fight, I guess, but there wasn't anyone around to punch. Not that it would've done any good, since there wasn't anyone to blame but myself. Damn, but I messed up."

"Can I help?" Mitch asked. There were any number of times he'd come to Ben for advice about something or other, including his feelings for Bethany. Most of his visits had been on the pretext of wanting a cup of coffee. It appeared that the tables were turned now, and if he could assist Ben in some way, then all the better.

"Help me? No." Ben shook his head and instantly seemed to regret the movement. He closed his eyes and waited a couple of moments before opening them again.

"You want me to make you breakfast?" Mitch asked. "I'm not a bad cook."

He couldn't tell whether Ben was taking his offer into consideration. Lowering his head, Ben mumbled something Mitch couldn't hear.

Mitch leaned closer. "Did you say something?"

"Have, ah...have you seen Bethany this morning?"

"No." He'd actually come to tell his friend what had happened between them last night and seek his advice.

"Have you tried phoning her?"

"No."

Ben gave a slight nod in the direction of the phone. "Go ahead, okay?"

Mitch checked his watch. "It's a little early, isn't it?"

"Maybe, but try, anyway."

Mitch wasn't keen on the idea. "Is there anything in particular you'd like me to ask her?"

Ben propped his elbows on the counter and covered his face with both hands. He rubbed his eyes, and when he glanced in Mitch's direction they seemed to glisten. "I didn't know," he said in a frayed whisper. "I...never knew."

"What didn't you know?" Mitch asked gently.

"Marilyn was pregnant."

Ben might as well have been speaking in a foreign language for all the sense he made. "And who's Marilyn?" Mitch asked in calm tones.

Ben dropped his hands. "Bethany's mother." He paused. "Bethany's my daughter. I'm the reason she came to Hard Luck, and when she told me...I pretended I never knew any Marilyn."

"You mean—"

"Yes," Ben shouted, and pounded his fist on the counter, hard enough for his hand to bounce away from the surface. "I'm Bethany's father."

Mitch swore under his breath.

"It was the shock. I...I never guessed. Maybe I should have...I don't know."

Mitch's mind buzzed with the information. He sat on the stool next to Ben, feeling the weight of his friend's burden as if it were his own.

"When she told me, I denied ever knowing her mother and then—" his face contorted with guilt "—I said some things I regret and sent Bethany away." Ben wiped impatiently at his eyes. "She ran out of here, and now I'm afraid she won't be back."

"I'll talk to her if you like." Although Mitch was happy to make the offer, he didn't know if he'd be a help or a hindrance. His own track record with Bethany wasn't exactly impressive.

"Would you?" Ben clung to Mitch's offer like a lifeline in a storm-tossed sea.

"Sure." Mitch needed to see her for his own reasons, anyway. "I'll do it right away," he said, eager now to find her. They'd parted on such cool terms Bethany might not be as eager for his company. But Mitch was willing to risk her displeasure. She needed him. When he'd been in pain and grief, she'd been there to comfort him. Ben's rejection must have left her reeling. Mitch suddenly understood how important it was to be the one to console her.

"Tell her..." Ben hesitated, apparently not knowing how to convey his message. "Tell her..." he began a second time, his voice weak. His eyes brightened again and he drew in a deep, shuddering breath. "That I'm proud to have her as my daughter."

To Mitch's way of thinking, Bethany would be better off hearing those words from Ben herself.

MITCH LEFT the café, and Ben was alone once again to deal with the pain and the guilt that had accompanied him most of the night. Even the brandy hadn't dulled the shock.

He had a daughter.

Even now, the words felt awkward on his tongue. Getting used to the idea was going to require some doing. What bothered him most was the thought of Marilyn's struggling alone, without him. It stung a little to know she'd married someone else so soon after his departure. But he couldn't blame her. What was she to do, pregnant with his child and unable to let him know?

Even if he'd learned the truth, he didn't think he could have helped her the way she needed. He might have been able to marry her. Maybe that could've been arranged. But he was involved in a war, and it wasn't like he could call time-out while he dealt with his personal problems. The navy wouldn't have released him from his obligations because he got a college girl pregnant.

If there was any single thing Ben regretted most about the past, it was returning Marilyn's letter unopened. It pained him almost to the point of being physically ill to think about her alone and pregnant, believing he didn't care. The truth of the matter was that he'd loved her deeply. It had taken him years to put his love for her behind him.

She'd done the right thing in marrying this other man, he decided suddenly. Ben wouldn't have been a good husband for her, or for any woman. He was too stubborn, too set in his own ways. "It was easier to comfort himself with those reassurances, he supposed, than deal with all the might-have-beens.

The fact was, he'd fathered this child. Except that Bethany wasn't exactly a child. She was an adult, and a mighty fine one at that. Any man would be proud to call her daughter.

Bethany. Ben would give anything to take back the things he'd said to her. It was the shock. The fear, too, of her wanting something from him when he had nothing to give—emotionally or financially. He couldn't change the past or make up to Marilyn and Bethany for what he'd done—and hadn't done.

Ben poured himself a second cup of coffee in an attempt to clear his head. His temples still throbbed—enough to convince him not to seek his solution in a bottle again anytime soon.

There was a knock at the front door. He'd forgotten that he'd left it locked. With a decided lack of enthusiasm, he shuffled across the café and unlatched the bolt. To his surprise, he found it was Mitch.

"She's gone," Mitch announced, sounding like a man in a trance.

"Bethany gone? What do you mean, gone?"

"I just saw Christian. Duke flew her out this morning."

Pain shot through Ben's chest and he felt the sudden need to sit down. He'd only just found her and now—now he'd lost her.

THE PIZZA HAD HELPED, Bethany decided, but not nearly enough. Sorry that Mariah had decided not to join her, after all, she sat on top of the big hotel bed in front of the television. She was halfheartedly watching a movie she'd seen before she'd left for Alaska and paying the same price now as she had in a California theater.

Earlier in the day, she'd had her hair trimmed, and while she was at it, she'd sprung for a manicure.

Following that, she'd found a shopping mall and lingered for hours, just poking about the shops and watching the people. It didn't take long, however, for the doubts and regrets to crowd their way back into her mind.

She'd ruined everything. With Ben feeling the way he did, she wasn't comfortable returning to Hard Luck, and at the same time she couldn't leave. Not with everything between her and Mitch still unresolved. If the situation had been different, she could have phoned her parents, but of course neither of them knew the real reason she'd accepted the teaching assignment in Alaska. She hadn't wanted them to know.

What about Chrissie? And Susan and Scott and Ronnie . . . She couldn't leave her students or break the terms of her contract. She had a moral and a legal obligation to the people who'd hired her. The state and the town had entrusted her with these young lives. She couldn't just walk out and leave.

On the other hand, how could she return? It was all she could do not to bury her face in her hands and weep. Even now, she didn't know what had possessed her to confront Ben with the truth last night. Her timing couldn't have been worse. The information had come at him with the stealth and suddenness of a bomb, exploding in his life. She hadn't prepared him in any way to learn she was his daughter.

No wonder he— Her thoughts came to a crashing halt at the loud knock on her door.

"Bethany."

"Mitch?"

"Please open up."

She hadn't a clue how he'd learned where she was staying. She scrambled off the bed and ran to unlatch the door.

He stood on the other side as though he was surprised he hadn't been forced to kick the door open. He blinked, then blurted, "Don't leave."

"Leave?" She followed his gaze to her small suitcase.

"You've packed your things."

True, but only for a short stay in Fairbanks. She wondered where Mitch thought she was going. Then she realized he must think she wasn't planning to return. That was it. He assumed she was leaving for good.

"Give me one good reason to stay," she invited.

He walked past her and into the room. As he moved, he shoved his fingers through his hair and inhaled sharply. Unable to stand still, he paced the area like a man possessed.

"I love you, and I'm not saying it because there's another man wanting to dance with you. I'm saying it because I can't imagine living without you." He stopped, his eyes imploring. "I need you, Bethany. I didn't realize how much until I found you gone."

"You love me?"

"I haven't given you much reason to believe that, have I? There are reasons . . . I know you don't want to listen to excuses, and I don't blame you. Bethany, I'm not saying any of this for Chrissie. I need you for *me*. I love you for *me*." He paused and dragged in an uneven breath.

All at once it didn't seem fair to mislead him any further. "I'm not going anywhere," she confessed. "I was coming back, and when I did, I planned to try to work all this out with you."

He closed his eyes as if a great weight had been lifted from him.

"I need to settle matters with someone else, too," she said.

"Ben." His eyes held hers. "He wants to talk to you."

Bethany struggled for a moment to control her emotions before she asked, "He told you?"

Mitch nodded. "You're his daughter."

"He admitted that?" Her eyes welled with tears.

Again he nodded.

"Is he all right? I shouldn't have said anything—you don't know how much I regret it." She found it difficult to maintain her composure. "It was unfair to confront him the way I did. I can only imagine what he must think. Please," she begged, "tell him I don't expect anything of him. I realized he lied, but I understand. I don't blame him. Who knows what any of us would have done in similar circumstances."

"He very badly wants to talk to you himself."

"He doesn't need to say a word. I understand. Please assure him for me that I don't want anything from him," she said again.

"You can tell him yourself. He's here."

"Here?"

"Actually he's downstairs in the bar waiting. We tossed a coin to see which of us got to speak to you first. I won."

He gestured at the bed. "Please sit," he instructed. "This seems to be a time for confessions." Bethany obediently perched on the edge of the mattress and looked up at him expectantly.

"There's something important you need to know about me," he said. "I should have told you sooner—I'm sorry I didn't. After I've told you, you can decide what you want to do. If you'd rather not see me again . . . well, you can decide that later."

"Mitch, what is it?"

He couldn't seem to stay in one place. "I love you, Bethany," he said urgently. "I'm not a man who loves easily. There's only been one other woman I've ever felt this strongly about."

"Your wife," she guessed.

"I—I don't know where to start." Mitch threw her a look of anguish.

"Start at the beginning," she coaxed gently, patiently. She'd waited a long time for Mitch to trust her enough with his past.

He resumed his pacing. "I met Lori while we were in college. I suppose our history was fairly typical. We fell in love and got married. I joined the Chicago Police Department, and our lives settled down to that of any typical young couple. Or so I thought."

He paused, and it seemed to Bethany that the light went out of his eyes.

"I see," she said quietly. "Go on."

Moving to stand in front of her, he said, "Chrissie was born, and I was crazy about her from the first. Lori wanted to be a good mother. I believe that, and she tried. She honestly tried. But she was accustomed to being in the workforce and mingling with other people, and staying home with the baby didn't suit her. About this time, I was assigned to Narcotics. From that point, my schedule became erratic. I rarely knew from one week to the next what my hours would be."

He stared somewhere above her head, as if the telling of these details was too painful to do directly.

"Lori became depressed. She saw a physician about it, and he explained that new-mother blues were fairly common. He prescribed something to help her feel better. He also gave her tranquilizers. A light dose to take when she had trouble sleeping."

"Did they help?"

"For a while, but then Lori found she couldn't sleep nights at all. It didn't help that Chrissie suffered from repeated ear infections, and Lori had to stay awake with her so often."

He frowned. "I don't know when she started doubling up on the tranquilizers, or even how she was able to get so many of them. I suspect she went to a number of different doctors."

Bethany held out her hand to him and Mitch gripped it hard between both of his own. Then he sat on the bed beside her, turning his body to face her. "What's so tragic about all this is that time and time again Lori told me how unhappy she was, how miserable. She didn't like being home. She didn't like staying with the baby so much. She wanted me home more often. She clung to me until I felt she was strangling me, and all along she was so terribly sick, so terribly depressed."

"Did you know she was hooked on the tranquilizers?"

"I suppose I guessed. But I didn't want to deal with it. I couldn't. I was working day and night on an important case," he said, his eyes bleak with his sorrow. "If she wanted to dope herself up at night with tranquilizers, then fine. I'd deal with it when I could, but not then." He closed his eyes and shook his head. "You see, I might have saved her life had I dealt with the problem immediately, instead of ignoring it and praying she'd snap out of it herself."

"What happened?" Bethany asked. She intuitively realized there was more to the story, and that it would only grow worse.

"If the signs had been any plainer, they would've hit me over the head."

"It happens every day."

"I worked with addicts. I should have known."

It was clear this was one thing Mitch would never forgive himself for.

"She killed herself," he said in a stark whisper. "Her family thought it was an accident, but I know better. She needed me, but I was too involved in chasing down a drug dealer to help my own wife. She was depressed, unhappy, miserable, and addicted to tranquilizers. I'm convinced she felt she had nothing left to live for. Certainly not a caring, tender husband. I turned my back on my own wife. I might as well have poured the pills down her throat."

"Oh, Mitch, you were under so much stress yourself. You can't blame yourself for Lori's weakness."

"Yes, I can," he said, "and I have. I should've realized what was happening to her. She paid the penalty for my neglect—with her life. I can understand if you don't want to marry me..."

"Is that what you're asking me, Mitch? To be your wife?"

"Yes." His gaze held hers. "I realize how much Chrissie loves you, but like I told you last night, it isn't for my daughter I'm asking. It's for me."

The lump in Bethany's throat refused to dissolve. She nodded and swallowed back her tears.

"Is that a yes?" he asked in a harsh whisper, as if he was afraid of the answer.

She nodded vigorously.

Mitch briefly closed his eyes. "I live a simple life, Bethany. I don't want to leave Hard Luck."

"I don't want to leave, either. My home is wherever you are."

"You're sure? Because I don't think I could let you go. Not now." He reached for her and kissed her with a hunger and a longing that left her breathless. A long time passed before he released her.

"We'd better stop while I've got the strength to let you go," he told her. "Besides, Ben's waiting."

"Ben." She'd almost forgotten.

"He's downstairs bragging to the bartender about his daughter," Mitch said with the hint of a smile. "Would you like to join him there? I know he wants to talk to you."

"In a little while," she whispered and pressed her head against his shoulder. They'd both come to Hard Luck for a purpose. His had been to hide; hers had been to locate the man whose genes she shared. Together they'd discovered something far more precious than the gold that had drawn generations of prospectors to Alaska.

Together they'd found each other. And love.

EPILOGUE

HALF AN HOUR LATER, Bethany made her way into the dimly lit cocktail lounge and found Ben sitting alone at a table, nursing a bottle of beer. His shoulders slumped forward and his head was bowed. It looked, she thought sadly, as if the weight of nearly thirty years of regret rested solidly on his back.

He raised his eyes to meet hers when she walked over to his table. "Do you mind if I sit down?" she asked, feeling tentative herself. She understood now that the way she'd confronted Ben had been a mistake; she wished more than anything that they could start over again.

He nodded, his expression concerned as she slid out the chair and sat across from him.

"Do you want something to drink?" he asked.

"No, thanks." The wine and brandy last night had loosened her tongue. She didn't want to repeat *that* mistake. "I'm so very sorry..."

"I'm the one who's sorry," Ben cut in. "I'm not proud of the way I reacted yesterday—my only excuse is shock."

"I couldn't have done a worse job of it," she said.

His face tightened, and his eyes grew suspiciously bright. "It's so hard to believe I could have a daughter as beautiful as you, Bethany. My heart feels like it's going to burst wide open just looking at you."

Bethany smiled tremulously, close to tears herself.

"Your mother... the resemblance between you is striking. I didn't see it at first, but I do now." He took a swallow of his beer and Bethany suspected he did it to hide his emotion. He set the bottle back on the table. "How is Marilyn? The cancer?"

"She's better than ever, and there's no sign of the cancer recurring."

"She's... she's had a good life? She's happy?"

Bethany nodded. "Very happy. Mom and Dad have a good marriage. Like any relationship, it's had its ups and downs over the years, but they're deeply in love, and they're truly committed to each other." She paused and drew in a deep breath. "They don't know that I've—that I found you."

He lowered his head. "Do you plan on telling them?"

"Yes, and you can be assured I'll handle it a lot more delicately than I did with you. I accepted the teaching contract in Hard Luck because I knew you were here, but originally I'd never intended to tell you."

"Not tell me?"

"All I wanted was to get to know you, but once I'd done that, it didn't seem to be enough. We're very alike, Ben, in many important ways. But before I knew that, I was afraid of the kind of man you'd be."

He sipped from the beer bottle. "I'm probably a disappointment..."

"No," she rushed to tell him. "No! I'm *proud* to be your daughter. You're a warm, generous, caring human being. Hard Luck Café is the heart of the community, and that's because of you."

"I can't be your father," Ben murmured with regret, "Your mother's husband—Peter—he'll always be that."

"That's true. But you could be my friend."

His face brightened. "Yes. A special friend."

Bethany stretched her hand across the table and Ben squeezed her fingers. "Where's Mitch?"

"He's in the lobby waiting for us." Bethany smiled, and the happiness bloomed within her. "This seems to be a day for clearing the air."

Ben placed some money on the table and together they walked out of the lounge. "Are you going to marry that young buck and put him out of his misery?"

"Oh, yes. I came to Hard Luck wanting to meet you, and instead I found *two* men I'll love all my life."

Mitch hurried toward them, and they met him halfway. Grinning widely, Ben slung an arm around their shoulders, drawing them close. "Well, my friends. This seems to be an evening to celebrate. Dinner's on me!"

* * * * *

In February, Matt Caldwell—who's soon to be Charles O'Halloran's brother-in-law—is determined to reconcile with Karen, his ex-wife. Especially when he finds out what Karen's been keeping from him! Watch for BECAUSE OF THE BABY, the fourth book in Debbie Macomber's MIDNIGHT SONS series.

Harlequin Romance ®

brings you

How the West Was Wooed!

Harlequin Romance would like to welcome you
back to the ranch again in 1996 with Hitched!

The trail starts with Margaret Way and A FAULKNER
POSSESSION (#3391). Roslyn thinks she's put the
past and her youthful infatuation with rancher Marsh
Faulkner behind her. But Marsh wants a "trophy"
wife and Roslyn fits the bill—love doesn't enter into
it. Though Roslyn is tempted, she can't reconcile
herself to being just another Faulkner possession.

Available in January wherever Harlequin books
are sold.

MILLION DOLLAR SWEEPSTAKES (III)

No purchase necessary. To enter, follow the directions published. Method of entry may vary. For eligibility, entries must be received no later than March 31, 1996. No liability is assumed for printing errors, lost, late or misdirected entries. Odds of winning are determined by the number of eligible entries distributed and received. Prizewinners will be determined no later than June 30, 1996.

Sweepstakes open to residents of the U.S. (except Puerto Rico), Canada, Europe and Taiwan who are 18 years of age or older. All applicable laws and regulations apply. Sweepstakes offer void wherever prohibited by law. Values of all prizes are in U.S. currency. This sweepstakes is presented by Torstar Corp., its subsidiaries and affiliates, in conjunction with book, merchandise and/or product offerings. For a copy of the Official Rules send a self-addressed, stamped envelope (WA residents need not affix return postage) to: MILLION DOLLAR SWEEPSTAKES (III) Rules, P.O. Box 4573, Blair, NE 68009, USA.

EXTRA BONUS PRIZE DRAWING

No purchase necessary. The Extra Bonus Prize will be awarded in a random drawing to be conducted no later than 5/30/96 from among all entries received. To qualify, entries must be received by 3/31/96 and comply with published directions. Drawing open to residents of the U.S. (except Puerto Rico), Canada, Europe and Taiwan who are 18 years of age or older. All applicable laws and regulations apply; offer void wherever prohibited by law. Odds of winning are dependent upon number of eligibile entries received. Prize is valued in U.S. currency. The offer is presented by Torstar Corp., its subsidiaries and affiliates in conjunction with book, merchandise and/or product offering. For a copy of the Official Rules governing this sweepstakes, send a self-addressed, stamped envelope (WA residents need not affix return postage) to: Extra Bonus Prize Drawing Rules, P.O. Box 4590, Blair, NE 68009, USA.

SWP-H1295

BRIDE'S BAY RESORT

UNLOCK THE DOOR TO GREAT ROMANCE AT BRIDE'S BAY RESORT

Join Harlequin's new across-the-lines series, set in an exclusive hotel on an island off the coast of South Carolina.

Seven of your favorite authors will bring you exciting stories about fascinating heroes and heroines discovering love at Bride's Bay Resort.

Look for these fabulous stories coming to a store near you beginning in January 1996.

Harlequin American Romance #613 in January
Matchmaking Baby by Cathy Gillen Thacker

Harlequin Presents #1794 in February
Indiscretions by Robyn Donald

Harlequin Intrigue #362 in March
Love and Lies by Dawn Stewardson

Harlequin Romance #3404 in April
Make Believe Engagement by Day Leclaire

Harlequin Temptation #588 in May
Stranger in the Night by Roseanne Williams

Harlequin Superromance #695 in June
Married to a Stranger by Connie Bennett

Harlequin Historicals #324 in July
Dulcie's Gift by Ruth Langan

Visit Bride's Bay Resort each month wherever Harlequin books are sold.

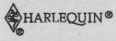

HARLEQUIN ®

BBAYG

Harlequin Romance ®

brings you

Some men are worth waiting for!

And next month, we kick off a new series with an all-American hero courtesy of ever-popular author Emma Goldrick. HUSBAND MATERIAL (#3392) is the story of local widow Rose Mary Chase who dreams of meeting the one man capable of sweeping her off her feet! A man like Sam Horton in fact—now there's a guy who would make a perfect husband. He's already a great dad to his young daughter, Penny. And Penny knows that what she and Sam need to make a perfect family is Rose!

Don't miss this first Holding Out for a Hero title. Available in January wherever Harlequin books are sold.

Harlequin Romance ®

New from Harlequin Romance a very special six-book series by

MIDNIGHT SONS

DEBBIE MACOMBER

The town of Hard Luck, Alaska, needs women!

The O'Halloran brothers, who run a bush-plane service called **Midnight Sons,** are heading a campaign to attract women to Hard Luck. *(Location: north of the Arctic Circle. Population: 150—mostly men!)*

"Debbie Macomber's *Midnight Sons* series is a delightful romantic saga. And each book is a powerful, engaging story in its own right. Unforgettable!"

—Linda Lael Miller

TITLE IN THE MIDNIGHT SONS SERIES:

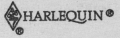